WINNER OF THE ILLA PRIZE 2023

'Like Flannery O'Connor and Juan Rulfo, Almada fills her (...) novels with an understanding of rural life, loneliness, temptation and faith.'
BBC Culture

'Almada's prose is sparse, but the details count. Her ear for dialogue and especially gossip is pitch perfect. Her eye for detail is hawkish.'
LA Review of Books

'Almada burns off all the dross and gives us pure revelation, cryptic and true.'
Paul Harding

'*Not a River* plunges us straight into the depths of its silences, bracingly so – the longer the quiet goes, the more terrible the rupture.'
Manuel Muñoz

'A powerful voice that emerges from the path forged by Juan Carlos Onetti and, further back, by William Faulkner and Erskine Caldwell.'
El País

'With incisive, lacerating writing that softens as the story progresses, Almada carries the reader to a place where pain, betrayal and fear are part of everyday life in the provinces.'
Le Monde

'I am a devoted reader of Selva Almada.'
Samanta Schweblin

NOT A RIVER

First published by Charco Press 2024
Charco Press Ltd., Office 59, 44-46 Morningside Road, Edinburgh
EH10 4BF

Work published with funding from the 'Sur' Translation Support Programme
of the Ministry of Foreign Affairs of Argentina / Obra editada en el marco
del Programa 'Sur' de Apoyo a las Traducciones del Ministerio de Relaciones
Exteriores y Culto de la República Argentina.

A CIP catalogue record for this book is available
from the British Library.

ISBN: 9781913867454
e-book: 9781913867461

www.charcopress.com

Edited by Fionn Petch
Cover designed by Pablo Font
Typeset by Laura Jones
Proofread by Fiona Mackintosh

2 4 6 8 10 9 7 5 3 1

Selva Almada

NOT A RIVER

Translated by
Annie McDermott

For Grillo, for all the years

See, my friend, the wealth of casuarina trees on the shore.
Now they are water.

Arnaldo Calveyra

Enero Rey, standing firm on the boat, stocky and beardless, swollen-bellied, legs astride, stares hard at the surface of the river and waits, revolver in hand. Tilo, the kid, aboard the same boat, leans back, the rod butt at his hip, turning the reel handle, tugging the line: a glittering thread in the waning sun. El Negro, fifty-something like Enero, alongside the boat, water up to his balls, leans back as well, red-faced from the sun and hard work, rod bent as he winds in and lets out the line. The spool spinning and his breath a kind of wheeze. The river pancake flat.

Pump and reel, pump and reel. She's hugging the bottom. Get her up, get her up.

After two, three hours, tired and almost through, Enero repeats the instructions in a murmur, like a prayer.

He feels dizzy. Pickled by the wine and heat. He looks up and his red eyes, sunk deep in his puffy face, are blinded and everything goes white and he's lost and reaches for his head and ends up firing into the air.

Without stopping what he's doing, Tilo grimaces and yells.

What the hell, you moron!

Enero comes to.

All good. You guys keep going. Pump and reel, pump and reel. She's hugging the bottom. Get her up, get her up.

She's coming! She's coming up!

Enero leans over the side. Sees it draw closer. A stain beneath the surface of the river. He takes aim and fires. Once. Twice. Three times. The blood rises, gushing, washes away. He sits up. Puts back the gun. Tucks it in the waistband of his shorts.

Tilo from the boat and El Negro from the water lift the creature out. Grabbing it by the fleshy grey frills. Throwing it on board.

Watch the stinger!

Says Tilo.

He takes the knife, cuts the barb from the body, sends it back to the depths of the river.

Enero sits down with a thud on the seat in the boat. Sweaty-faced, head buzzing. Drinks a little water from the bottle. It's warm, he drinks anyway, long gulps, then tips the rest over his head.

El Negro climbs in. The ray takes up so much space there's almost nowhere to put his feet without treading on it. Must be some two hundred pounds, maybe two hundred twenty.

Christ she's ugly!

Says Enero, slapping his thigh and laughing. The others laugh as well.

Fought us pretty hard.

Says El Negro.

Enero picks up the oars and rows into the middle of the river and then turns and carries on, following the shore around to where they'd set up camp.

They'd left town at dawn in El Negro's pickup. Tilo in the middle brewing the mate. Enero with his arm resting on the open window. El Negro at the wheel. They watched how the sun slowly climbed above the asphalt. Felt how the heat began to burn from early on.

They listened to the radio. Enero took a leak by the roadside. At a petrol station they bought pastries and filled up on hot water for the mate.

All three of them pleased to be hanging out together. They'd been planning the trip for a while now. With one thing and another it kept getting called off.

El Negro had bought a new boat and wanted to try it out.

While they were crossing to the island in the brand-new boat they remembered, as usual, the first time they'd brought Tilo, who was still only tiny then, barely even walking, and how they'd got caught in a storm, the tents blown to shit, and the kid, little pipsqueak that he was, wound up sheltering in the boat propped on its side among some trees.

Your old man had hell to pay when we got back.
Said Enero.

Again they told the story Tilo knows off by heart. How Eusebio smuggled the kid along without a word to Diana Maciel. He and Diana'd been split up pretty much since Tilo was born. Eusebio had him at weekends. And of course, that would be the weekend she realizes she's forgotten to pack, in the bag with his clean clothes, some medication Tilo was taking. Diana stops by the house and there's no one there. A neighbour tells her they've gone to the island.

And then the storm that tore through the whole area. The town as well. Diana with her heart in her mouth.

We were lucky, all of us.
Said Enero.

Diana Maciel had laid into the three of them hard and for weeks they were banned from seeing Tilo or setting foot in her house.

On reaching the camp, they unload the ray and run a rope through the slits behind its eyes and hang it from a tree. The three bullet holes merge with its mottled back. If their edges weren't paler, kind of pinkish, they'd look like part of the pattern.

Reckon I've earned myself a beer.

Says Enero.

He's sitting on the ground, his back to the tree and the ray. The buzzing in his head has stopped, but there's still a kind of knot there.

Tilo goes and opens the cooler and takes a bottle from the water, from among the last few floating ice cubes. He pops the cap with the lighter then passes it on, so that it's him, Enero Rey, the one who's earned it, who first brings the bottle to his lips. The beer hits his mouth, all foam that goes streaming over his lips, painting white lace on his jet-black moustache. Like rinsing his mouth out with cotton wool. Only with the second swig does the cool, bitter liquid come.

El Negro and Tilo sit down as well, all three in a row, the bottle moving from hand to hand.

Too bad we don't have a camera.

Says El Negro.

They all turn their heads to look at the creature.

It's like an old blanket hanging in the shade.

Midway through the second bottle, a gaggle of kids appear, dark and wiry as eels, their faces nothing but eyes. They crowd around the ray, jostling, shoving.

Wooooah. Check it out check it out. It's ginormous!

One grabs a stick and pokes it through the bullet holes.

Hey, hands off!

Says Enero, standing up suddenly, huge as a bear. And the little tykes scatter, vanishing back into the woods.

Since he's on his feet now, since he's made the effort to get up, Enero decides to go for a dip. The water clears his head.

He swims.

Ducks under.

Floats on the surface.

The sun's beginning to set and a slight breeze is creasing the river.

Just then he hears the engine and the lapping of waves. He moves aside, begins swimming to shore. The boat goes by, bounding over the water, ripping it in two like a rotten old rag. Attached to the back of the boat, a girl in a bikini is water-skiing. The boat swerves sharply and the girl is thrown in the water. From a distance, Enero sees her head emerge, her long hair plastered to her scalp.

He thinks of the Drowner.

Gets out.

El Negro and Tilo are standing on the shore, arms folded, following the boat with their eyes.

Youngsters making a racket.

Says El Negro.

It's the same every weekend. They scare the fish. Ought to give them a scare ourselves one of these days.

The three of them turn and come face-to-face with the men. They hadn't heard them approach. The islanders are light on their feet.

Afternoon.

Says the one who just spoke.

We heard from the kids and came to see. Beautiful animal!

The others are looking at the ray. Standing beside it, to measure it.

My name's Aguirre, says the only one who talks, and he holds out his hand, which they each shake.

Enero Rey, says Enero, joining the group and greeting them one by one. El Negro and Tilo follow, doing the same.

Pretty big, huh?

Says Enero and pats it on the flank, then recoils as if it had burnt him.

Aguirre, inspecting the holes from up close, says.

Three? You shot it three times. Once would've done.

Enero grins, showing the gap where he's missing a front tooth.

Guess I got carried away.

You want to watch that… getting carried away.

Says Aguirre.

Tilo, pour some wine for our pals here.

Says El Negro, stepping in between.

The boy runs to the shore, where they'd buried the demijohn to keep it cool. He brings it over and fills a tin cup to the brim.

He hands it to Aguirre, who raises it.

Cheers, he says and takes a swig and passes it to Enero. He looks for a moment at Enero's left hand, which is missing a finger, but doesn't ask any questions. Enero sees, but keeps quiet as well. Let him wonder.

Cristo here caught one way bigger the other day, Aguirre brags. How long were you out there?

All afternoon, the guy replies, with a sideways glance.

And how many times you shoot it?

Once. Once is enough.

See, my pal here's a bit of a klutz.

El Negro says and laughs.

The TV people came and all, says the guy who landed a bigger ray than this one. Put him on the evening news, says Aguirre. Last Saturday the place was teeming with folks from Santa Fe and Paraná. Thought it was rays galore here. Like it's that easy. You guys had some luck.

Technique, says Enero. Luck and technique. Luck alone won't get you far.

Aguirre takes a pouch of tobacco from the pocket of his shirt, which he wears unbuttoned, open over his bony chest, over his wine-swollen belly. He rolls in the blink of an eye. Lights up. Takes a puff as he wanders over to the shore and stands gazing out at the water. Then he looks back at them and says.

So how long you staying?

Two, three days, says El Negro. It's a nice island.

You're right there.

Says Aguirre.

El Negro steps into the woods. T-shirt slung over his shoulder, strides long but slow. Everything here in semi-darkness. Outside, the sun, a ball of fire half snuffed out by the river. He hears the soft sounds of birds and other small animals. A whisper of weeds.

Wild guinea pigs, weasels, viscachas scurrying through the tall grass. El Negro moves with care, with respect, as if entering a church. Dainty as a guazuncho deer. But of course he ends up treading on a twig, a bunch of curupí pods, and the result is deafening. The crackle of dry shells echoes through the alders and timbós, up and out of the dense circle of woodland. Announcing the presence of an intruder.

This man isn't from these woods and the woods are well aware. But they leave him be. He can come in, he can stay for as long as it takes to gather kindling. Then the woods themselves will spit him out, his arms full of branches, back to the shore.

El Negro's eyes begin to adjust and he makes out a camoati nest attached to a branch a bit farther on, like a head strung up by the hair. Around it the air quivers, thick with wasps.

He takes a deep breath and his chest fills with the scent of flowers, honey and the odd small dead animal. Everything smells sweet.

Distracted, he steps in a puddle and a cloud of mosquitoes fly up and surround him. Their high-pitched humming all he can hear. They prick at his back, his arms, his bare neck. He flaps his T-shirt, scaring them away. Then puts it on before they eat him alive.

Yeah, yeah, I'm going, I'm just getting some wood then I'm going.

He says aloud.

He collects a bundle of twigs to get the fire started. Knocks his head on a big hanging branch that's still just about clinging to the tree. He puts down what he's carrying. Tests the branch with his weight, pulls it free. The tearing wood makes a noise like the lightning that split it. He squats again, scoops up the twigs, tucks them under his arm. With his other hand he drags the heavy branch.

He emerges. The sky is orange, the air soupy and warm. A shiver runs down his spine to his backside. He turns, looks over his shoulder. He could swear the woods have closed up behind him.

Tilo is crouching on the ground, untangling a knotted line. His long, slight fingers move as if braiding the air. Cigarette stuck to his lip, one eye closed against the smoke. Enero watches him. Sits on the ground, cross-legged like an indio, and watches him. If he didn't know it was Tilo he'd say Eusebio had come back. If he couldn't see his own bulging belly, his pudgy hands, his stump, his greying chest hair, he'd say Tilo was Eusebio, who hadn't yet died. That the three of them were fishing again, just like back in the day.

He remembers it was their first summer together when he started dreaming about the Drowner.

He'd known El Negro since forever, but Eusebio had moved to their part of town not so long ago. That year, after the July vacation, he started at the school. The family had come to live in the grandma's house after the old lady died. Apparently they'd not been on good terms, which was why they'd never visited before. Their arrival didn't go down well with the neighbours. Some folks said Eusebio's dad had done time and the old lady had never forgiven him. And that Eusebio's mother saw men for money.

The three of them would meet each morning as soon as they got up, almost always at Enero's because he was an only child. They drank their milk and then they were off, sometimes not coming back till after dark. Most days they went to the dam. They liked lazing under the trees on the shore, fishing lines tied around their toes, waiting for something to bite. They chatted, read comics and flicked through the magazines full of naked women and crime stories that Eusebio brought from home.

They were eleven.

That morning he told them about his dream, but he didn't tell them he'd woken up screaming, or that he'd wet the bed. The Drowner's face pressed against his, the soft grey flesh, cheeks eaten away by the fish so you could see the line of molars. He'd grabbed him by the hair to push him away and been left with a clump in his fist.

El Negro had burst out laughing.

Yeah right.

He said.

But Eusebio had looked at him with interest.

So who was it?

He said.

Who was what, said Enero.

The drowned dude.

He just said he was all rotted away – it could've been anyone!

Said El Negro.

Enero nodded, as if to say, well, duh. Eusebio frowned and shrugged. Just then the line around his big toe gave a twitch and the three of them stared at the murky water, their heads together, and didn't mention the dream again that day.

Enero moves the stump of his finger, the pink tip that always seems covered in newborn skin, skin that never hardens. Thinner than the skin on the rest of his hand. A fresh growth, even now.

The finger went pretty much when Eusebio did. A few weeks after they buried his friend, his buddy, his brother. As if a part of him, real and concrete, had to die as well.

A finger.

Not much.

Pocket change.

In the siesta that day, he'd decided to clean his police firearm, wine-soaked as he was. Off his face and mad at the rookie cop who'd refused to give him a ride home in the patrol car.

What was his name again?

It's not a taxi service, the little tight-ass had said.

What was his name?

He didn't last long in the town. Soon got promoted. Requested a transfer. The wife couldn't get on with the place.

What was his name?

He'd gone crashing down on the brick floor under the awning. Before that, the smell of powder, the dizziness, everything spinning. Then the green flies and the sticky gunk all over his fingers, the four he had left. Who knows how long he was there, he doesn't remember. Then his mother's voice. The voice coming out of her room.

Tonio. Tonio, get in here. Don't make me beg or you won't get nothing from me.

The hoarse, syrupy voice. The cheeky giggle.

He never learned who Tonio was. Whether he'd screwed his mum before his dad, after, or during. But for Delia in those final years, before she slipped away completely, he wasn't Enero, he wasn't her son, just a series of names she tossed out between laughs: lovers, boyfriends, passing fancies, or just figments of her imagination.

Out of the woods now, El Negro stops to catch his breath. He sees the pair of them sitting on the ground, equidistant. Tilo a boy like they used to be. Enero a man like he is now, getting old like him. When did they stop being like that and start being like this?

He looks toward the shore. Swarms of mosquitoes shimmer like mirages above the water. By the last dusk light he sees them swirl in their dozens over Tilo's bowed head as the boy sits lost in thought. He sees them over Enero's body, too. His back is black with mosquitoes. He sees him raise his two brawny arms, rotate them slowly like the blades of a fan, scaring off the insects without spilling any blood. Something about that action moves him. Something about the sight of his two friends, the boy and the man, moves him. He feels the fire of the sunset caress his chest, from the inside out.

El Negro doesn't remember the second time Enero dreamed about the Drowner. He wasn't there when he told the story; his sisters had just shown up, wanting to take him home for a haircut. Enero, Eusebio and him were drinking tereré in the yard, under the awning. His sisters had shouted from the roadside, two of the five, who all looked the same, long hair, tall and slender as herons. Their voices were the same, too. Even he couldn't tell them apart.

Negrito. Negrito. Negrito.

They shrieked, till Delia came out to take control.

Go on, they're calling you. I can't watch the novela with this noise.

He always listened to Delia. That woman and his sisters were the closest thing to a mother he'd ever known. His own mother dead in the maternity ward. His father, a horse breaker, always on the road. Him alone with his sisters, who treated him like a doll.

Then once he'd left and Delia had finished her cigarette and flicked it into the plants and gone back inside, Enero told Eusebio he'd seen the Drowner again.

Enero was swimming in a stream when all of a sudden he felt something pulling him under. He swam harder, fighting to stay afloat, but that thing climbing his legs like a honeysuckle was too strong for him. He opened his eyes in the dirty water and there the guy was, clinging to him, tugging at his legs, dragging him down to the bottom. He tried to break free. But the Drowner's saggy skin went on wrapping around him, covering him like a cocoon. Again Enero woke up sopping wet, as if he really had just come out of the stream from his nightmare. That time he didn't shout for his mother, or wet the bed. He stayed still for a while, taking little gasping breaths, then curled up tight with his face to the wall.

Eusebio helped himself to the last of the tereré, the ice clinking inside the thermos.

Must be a sign.

He said.

How d'you mean.

Said Enero.

Eusebio looked at him and thought for a moment.

We need to go see my godfather. He knows about this stuff.

He said.

The wood burns, turning to embers.

When the embers are ready, El Negro spreads them under the grill. Lays the skirt steak on top. Some chorizos.

Enero and Tilo are playing cards. Old maid. A kids' game. If Enero ends up the old maid, Tilo laughs at him, teases him, like he's still a little kid. Enero chuckles and shakes his head.

Just you wait, just you wait. I'll wipe the floor with you next time.

El Negro lights a cigarette and heads for the shore.

The three of them went to see Eusebio's godfather. El Negro and Enero on their bikes, taking turns to give Eusebio a ride. They crossed the whole town, his house was a long way away, in a part they'd never been to, poorer than the neighbourhood where they grew up and which they hardly ever left. Dirt roads, stagnant water in the ditches, scrawny dogs lying in the shade of the shacks. It felt kind of creepy to be there in the middle of the day, when the shops close up and everyone goes home for a siesta. Not a soul outside in that heat.

When they reached his godfather's place, some people were gathered under a tarp that served as a makeshift porch. More women than men and kids with the women, fanning themselves with bits of magazines.

They're the customers.

Said Eusebio.

His godfather was a healer and he was called Gutiérrez.

Hang on a second.

He said and darted around the side of the shack.

The people watched him go and then eyed the two boys. Taking no chances, the pair hung back, waiting under the tree where they'd propped their bikes. El Negro was nervous: his sisters were Evangelicals and thought everything that wasn't God's work was the work of the devil. Healers like this, for example. If they found out where he was he'd get a hiding and a half. And Enero wasn't much calmer. The way Delia saw things, there wasn't God's work or the devil's, it was all just the same: stuff that suckers believed. Which was all very well, but every now and then when Enero asked Jesus for something, he got it. So what was he supposed to think.

Two kids had come over and one asked for the bikes.

To try them out.

He said.

Enero said no.

The kid whispered something to his friend and they laughed. Then he spat on the ground and they turned and went off back to where the grown-ups were waiting.

The meat's starting to cook and you can smell it. The chorizo fat sizzling on the embers. El Negro comes back and sits nearby. Keeps an eye on the fire. Takes a swig of his wine.

By the light of the flames, he sees the ray. Feels surprised, like he hadn't expected it to be there, hanging from the tree where they left it a few hours before. He laughs. Where would it have gone? Then he looks at it again. Stands up and moves closer. Studies it. Touches it. The skin is dry, tight. The flesh slightly warm. He smells it. It smells of mud. Of river. He shuts his eyes and keeps sniffing. Behind those odours, another is beginning that he doesn't like.

He straightens up, steps back and studies it some more. Shaking his head. What are they going to do with the creature? If they leave it here, it'll rot in the dew and by noon the next day there'll be two hundred pounds of gone-off meat hanging from the tree.

Enero's snort of laughter, thunderous.

What did I tell you, kiddo? What did you expect? Enero's the king. Enero Rey. Clue's in the name, son.

Tilo's laugh, softer, more like his dad's.

The king, sure. The king of getting your ass kicked.

Hey.

Says El Negro.

Hey.

He repeats.

His friends turn to look, the laughter still on their faces.

El Negro points at the animal, at the mottled hide, as if pointing at a map.

What we gonna do with this?

He asks.

They waited hours that day. Being the healer's godson didn't get you special treatment. Eusebio kept going back and forth to the house, returning with mortadella sandwiches given him by his godmother, and cool water fresh from the well. Enero had a quick nap. El Negro wanted to take a dump and had to go behind some bushes. After one of those trips to the house, when just about everyone had left, Eusebio came running back and told them to hurry, that his godfather would see them now.

They went into a tiny room that smelt of hot wax. Red candles were burning everywhere. In the middle of a table, a tall, thin man sitting in a chair with armrests, and another chair, this one empty. The man was Gutiérrez. He had his legs crossed like a woman and he was smoking, holding the cigarette between two fingers as long and thin as the rest of him. His fingernails were long as well. He told them to come closer. Enero stepped forward, but El Negro hovered by the door.

So you're Enero.

The guy said.

Enero nodded.

And you've been dreaming about the Drowner.

Enero looked at Eusebio, who answered for him.

Like twice already.

He said.

Come here, sit down.

Said Gutiérrez.

Enero did as he was told. The man left the cigarette in the ashtray and laid his hands on the table. He wiggled his fingers, signalling for Enero to give him his, then took hold of them and shut his eyes. He pulled him a bit, bringing him closer. Enero could smell the wine on his breath. The man kept him there a few moments and then let go as if he'd been burnt. He leant back in his chair and returned to his cigarette. A curl of ash had formed, like a scab, which fell off with the movement.

Sometimes dreams are echoes of the future.

Said Gutiérrez.

You'll be dreaming about him forever, so you'd better get used to it.

Enero's belly turned to ice and he thought he might puke.

The healer gave a sideways nod and Eusebio took Enero by the arm and led him out. El Negro, the closest to the door, was the first to open it. The healer tutted at him.

Negrito, you've got worms, that's why you're so skinny. Eat a clove of garlic before breakfast every morning for a week.

El Negro shot him a glance and then hurried outside. Eusebio and Enero followed.

Tilo fiddles with the dial of the little battery-powered radio.

White noise. Static. An Evangelical preacher. Static. The lottery. Commercials. White noise. Tropical music.

Leave it. Leave it.

Says Enero, reaching an arm out to stop him. The hand at the end of that arm sways gently, in time with his head, his smiling face. His face lighting up with that smile. Enero manoeuvres his body, heaves it off the ground and settles it on his legs, his bare feet plump as empanadas. His other arm pushing at the air. One bringing it closer, the other pushing it away. One bringing it closer, the other pushing it away. His hips move, forward and back, forward and back, a gentle rocking. His face lifted to the starry night. Mouth open in a grin. The moon illuminating his missing tooth. Tilo joins in. Takes hold of one of Enero's hands with his fingertips. Tilo's legs, skinny like a bird's, like a heron's, snap forward and back. Enero spins him, pulls him back in, slides one arm around his waist. Their hips meet, finding a rhythm. Forward and back. Now the bodies, pressed together, push the air away. Bring it closer. Push it away. Enero sings. Throws his head back and sings. Tilo breaks free and dances beside him as Enero sings, adding his voice to the one coming from the radio. El Negro claps along. The lit cigarette in his mouth. He puffs, exhales. Puffs, exhales. His free hands clapping along.

Enero holds one fist to his mouth. Singing like it's a mic. Shuts his eyes. Impassioned. Tilo dances. Now just one leg in front, shaking his hips, twirling slowly. Arms barely moving. Enero goes to where El Negro's sitting on the ground and clapping. The singer leans down, holds his fist between El Negro's mouth and his own. El Negro joins in. Enero straightens up, and with his free hand beckons El Negro to the stage. Tilo reaches out to him, bouncing up and down, pulling him by the hand, and El Negro clambers to his feet.

The three of them dance.

Tilo, cocky, plucks the cigarette from El Negro's mouth and takes a drag.

Enero Rey wakes with a full bladder. He's sleeping outside the tent, on a mat laid under the trees, under the starry sky. He gets up and goes to the shore. The jet comes out like a blessing, hits the surface of the water. Enero lifts his head, the yawn opening his mouth. Enough stars to make you dizzy. The moon, still bright at the centre of the night.

He finishes, shakes himself dry, tucks his dick in his shorts. Yawns again. This time with a kind of bleat. He can't muster a howl.

You're not a werewolf any more, Enero. You're a sheep.

A summer like this one. Twenty years back, a summer like this one. The same island or the next one along or the one after that. In the memory it's all just the island, with no name or exact coordinates.

The island.

The three of them men by then. Not striplings like Tilo now. Men pushing thirty. Single. No plans to get hitched. Not one of them had plans to get hitched. At least at that point not one of them had plans to get hitched. Why should they. They had each other. And besides, Enero had his mother; El Negro had the sisters who'd raised him; Eusebio could have whoever took his fancy. Why get tied down to one if he could have them all. And so, at thirty, the three of them in the sun on the shore. Their brains on fire.

They'd left the dance at seven in the morning, pretty hammered.

What d'you say we go fishing?

Let's do it.

They tossed the three sleeping mats in El Negro's pickup. No tent, no point, it's baking, they're young and strong, what do they need with a tent. The rods, the net.

The Styrofoam cooler. Two demijohns of wine. A pan to fry whatever they caught. A bunch of painkillers for their fuggy heads.

They left their going-out clothes in Enero's bathroom, balled up on the floor. Enero gave them some shorts and old T-shirts. His mother rinsed her mouth with the first mate of the day and then followed them out, thermos under her arm, brewing them more so they didn't set off with nothing in their bellies but wine.

At the edge of town they stopped at the service station to buy ice and fill the tank. The smell of gasoline turned El Negro's stomach. He ran off, past the pumps, and puked onto the grass.

The attendant laughed.

Big night last night? And now you're headed to the island.

That's right.

Said Enero, at the wheel. Eusebio was snoring, his head tipped back, his whole mouth hanging open.

The fish biting out there?

So they say.

Said Enero with a shrug.

Maybe I'll swing by Sunday, then.

El Negro returned. His head wet, his longish hair dripping.

All good?

Yup.

Enero reached out the window and the attendant gave him a high five. He started the engine. They pulled away. Then he slammed on the brakes.

The ice!

The cool of the river, as the boatman took them across, began to wake them up. They didn't say anything. The old man was talking to himself. Because he had no teeth or because he was used to talking to himself, they could only make out the odd phrase.

Back then Enero was dreaming a lot about the Drowner. Maybe that, or maybe the tail-end of his hangover, was why he kept staring at the brownish water. As if expecting to see that slimy skull go bobbing past the boat. The hair all rotten, floating like white roots.

The three of them lost in thought. The old man's voice cracking.

Later on, all three refreshed by a swim in the river, stretched out on the shore, gleaming like bream, the sun scorching their backs.

Might as well fight fire with fire.

Said Enero, getting to his feet.

He pulled a demijohn from the ice, opened it, filled the tin cups, buried it again.

They stood and clinked cups.

I'm having a kid.

Said Eusebio.

Enero snorted with laughter. He laughed with his mouth open, still full of teeth. El Negro joined in with a nervous chuckle. Eusebio smiled and looked at the ground.

I'm serious, dumbass. What's so funny.

You, a kid. Who with?

Diana, who d'you think.

They looked at each other.

El Negro gave him a hug.

Enero took a long swig of wine and then clapped him on the back. A gesture half-congratulating, half-consoling.

A kid.

He murmured.

He laughed again. With happiness this time. Raising his glass. The noon sun glinted on the metal. Once more they drank to the kid Eusebio was having.

The kid.

The guys are still asleep. The animal's skin shines in the moonlight. Enero makes up his mind, gets the knife and cuts the ropes that keep it hanging from the tree, heaves it onto his shoulder, shifts the warm mushy body against his own. Wrinkles his nose. It's beginning to smell rank.

He wades a little way through the water to the boat. Hefts the creature on board. Again the animal takes up so much space, all the space there is. He doesn't want to tread on it. The thought of sinking into that flesh makes him feel sick. He adjusts it some more, kind of folding it over, making room for himself.

He begins to row out into the river. The poor thing weighs a ton.

Unlike his mother. Frail as a leaf in her final days. Her body a bundle of dry chirca twigs held together by her nightdress. She looked so small to Enero, lying in bed, and he wondered how a big guy like himself could've come out of a such a tiny body. Sometimes he said this to her and she laughed.

As if you're my son! I never had you inside me, but I wouldn't say no.

When he sends it overboard, the creature returns to the river without a sound. Some ripples form on the surface and that's that. It sinks back to where it came from.

The boat, lighter now, rocks gently.

The night is huge.

Enero feels in his shorts pocket for the pack of cigarettes with the lighter inside. He takes it out and pokes with a finger to see if any are left. He finds one, right in the corner. Lights it. Takes a drag. Looks at the water. It's still calm.

Beneath the boat, the river is blacker than the night.

When Eusebio went missing it was the divers who found him. The river there is thick as tar. You can't see a thing underwater. The men have to search by feel.

El Negro wanting to help.

Enero wanting to help.

The islanders wanting to help.

But no.

Leave it to the experts.

You guys had your chance to find him.

Said the officer.

The reproach, or explanation, or both, hung in the air. Time for the people who know what they're doing to take over, was what he meant.

But not what he said.

And Enero got angry.

It was like he was blaming them.

How could the officer understand when he didn't even know them. When he didn't know Eusebio. Or El Negro. When he had no idea how close they were.

When he had no idea that if one of them went, he took part of the other two with him.

They waited hour after hour on the shore. Smoking. Rubbing their arms through their shirts. It wasn't cold. It was just a feeling.

He and El Negro stared at the divers as they worked. Some in the boats. Others in the river, going under, coming up, the water like ink. Dark, thick. Like ink.

The divers wearing wetsuits, goggles. The ones going in. The others holding the rope that connects the divers beneath the surface to those on the boat. One with a walkie-talkie.

The ones in wetsuits going under, coming up. The water dark, thick. No sign.

Enero could feel a lump in his throat.

That feeling would never leave him. That grief. It still hits him from time to time. It hits him right now as he's smoking by himself.

In the middle of the river.

In the middle of the night.

They didn't expect to see Aguirre again. But here he is this morning, in the flesh, as they're sitting drinking mate around the fire.

He appears suddenly, out of the woods. Tilo sees him first and gives a start. Jerking his head, he signals to the others. El Negro and Enero slowly turn to look.

Aguirre is with them in no time. He stops, hands on hips, cigarette dangling from his mouth. The ash curls like a bagworm.

Morning.

Says El Negro.

Aguirre looks at them and then at the tree where he remembers the ray hanging. Just yesterday.

He looks at the tree.

Looks at them.

Looks at the tree.

Morning.

He eventually replies.

With what seems to be a well-practised motion, he switches the cigarette from one side of his mouth to the other. The ash drops. A little gets stuck on the shirt that bulges over Aguirre's belly.

Tilo, tasked with brewing the mate, offers some to him.

Aguirre accepts.

We never turn down a mate on this island. Not even from an enemy.

He spits out his cigarette. Looks back at the tree. Looks at the other trees nearby as well, not quite trusting his memory.

As he's drinking the mate, he nods in that direction.

What did you do?

He says at last.

The guys exchange glances.

Enero shrugs.

It smelt rank.

He says, abrupt.

Aguirre hands back the mate gourd. Shifts uneasily on his feet. Looks at the tree again, looks at the river. Looks at the river some more.

No one speaks. Tilo, kind of scared, looks at Enero and El Negro.

Aguirre rolls a cigarette. Runs his tongue along the paper. Spits out a strand of tobacco.

You should've said yesterday.

He says.

Enero gets to his feet.

You guys should've said if you wanted it.

He says.

Aguirre holds his gaze.

Enero doesn't flinch. He's pissed off. You can tell.

Aguirre, at that moment, lights his cigarette.

Everything's so quiet, so still, that you can hear the crackle as the paper and tobacco burn away.

Aguirre smiles.

He seems about to say something, but doesn't say it.

Instead, he says.

Fix me another mate, kid. For the road.

After two, three mates, Aguirre returns to the woods he emerged from. Enero looks at El Negro and whistles through his teeth. El Negro shakes his head.

Forget it.

He says.

These people are like that. You never know what's going through their heads.

Ask around and anyone in town will remember Eusebio's accident. The first stirrings: sounds like someone's gone missing, there's a search on. Then the panic: what if it was this person or that, plenty of folks were out fishing that weekend, it was a national holiday, the beginning of summer, word was the fish were frolicking in the river like butterflies. The rumours narrowing down: Eusebio Ponce. Eusebio from the motorbike repair shop. Ponce, the father of Diana Maciel's kid. Some wives and relatives breathing a sigh of relief: oh, it's Eusebio, from someone else's family, not mine, father to someone else's child, not mine. But then the prayer chains even so, because maybe today it wasn't me but in a small town a tragedy's everyone's business, we're all mixed up together around here.

Delia and El Negro's sisters distraught. Eusebio was like a son. A brother. What if it had been their son, their brother? What if the rumours are wrong, if they've got the wrong guy?

If it's Enero.

If it's El Negro.

By then Delia's mind was on the way out, and yet that day, for all those hours till the body was found, she seemed perfectly lucid again. The lady who used to sit with her when Enero was at work or off fishing hadn't said a word, but somehow the sly old fox knew. She, who had never believed in anything, sent the lady to buy candles and then they lit the entire pack. The lady had added a San Cayetano prayer card she always carried in her purse because there wasn't a single Christ, or crucifix, or anything, in the house.

Pray, since you know how, Delia had ordered her.

The lady, who wasn't all that devout herself, but knew the Lord's Prayer and the Hail Mary, began to pray. The two women sitting at the kitchen table, the plate of candles between them, the prayer card propped against a cup. Delia copied her, childlike, clasping her hands and moving her lips. The woman glanced at her and smiled.

You silly old thing, as if anyone could fool God.

El Negro's sisters found out when one of them went into town, to buy fabric to make some dresses. The guy in the shop brought it up.

Hey, you know how your brother's always off fishing.

Her hand had flown to her throat. She felt strangled, breathless, her stomach in knots. She left the shopkeeper with the cloth laid out on the counter, before she'd decided between the pastel muslin and the floral viyella. She left him ruler in hand, the scissors poised among the rolls, their blades open like a hummingbird's beak. And she fled. The Turk watched her go and cursed his loose tongue: if only he'd held off a bit, made the sale and then the comment.

She arrived home flushed and frantic.

The others were drinking mate and leafing through magazines. The twin sister of the girl who'd just got back sprang to her feet. When one was frightened, so was the other. Like a delayed mirror image, she too reached for her throat, felt the strangled sensation, the shortness of breath, the knot in her stomach. The other three stared.

Jesus Christ, what happened?

Said the eldest.

Then right away they went to see the pastor.

It was a Saturday, early afternoon. The man was only just up from his siesta. His wife glared when she saw them arrive. She didn't like those sisters, always hanging around the church. So single, so appealing. Then she sat next to her husband with the thermos and mate gourd.

Didn't offer any to the girls. The pastor listened to them with his head on one side. Twice his wife slurped loudly through the mate straw and her husband gave her a look, asking her to show some respect.

I'll get some fresh leaves.

She said and went off.

The pastor told them to calm down.

The good Lord will show us the way.

He said.

We need to trust in Him.

While the pastor went to wash his face and put on a shirt, the girls opened the drapes in the church – the pastor's garage, where there was a small stage made of wooden pallets, two speakers, a pulpit, and maybe thirty plastic chairs in stacks. They drew back the drapes and began setting out the chairs.

Diana Maciel hunkered down in one of the hotel rooms. She was the owner of the only hotel in town, a big old house, with several rooms and shared bathrooms, used mostly by travelling salesmen. The town never got tourists. There was nothing there to see.

That weekend Tilo was off in the country with his godmother, Marisa Soria, Diana's best friend. Someone came and told Diana the news.

Eusebio's gone missing on the river.

He said.

When the man left, Diana asked the maid to keep an eye on things. She took two packs of cigarettes and shut herself in the room she almost never rented out. She kept it for herself, for when she wanted to be alone or the rare times she brought someone back.

It had the best view, overlooking a part of the garden full of red China roses. When they were in bloom she had to close the shutters because all those flowers together gave her a headache. She lay on the bed with the ashtray on her belly. Planning to stay put and wait for the news. Not of Eusebio's death, she knew he was dead, there was no hope, the guy had told her. The news that the body had been found.

Before shutting herself in the room she'd called Marisa Soria. She explained the situation and then right away she told her not to cry. Normally the slightest thing set Marisa off, but she had to hold it together so she could look after Tilo. She heard her do some breathing exercises. Then came her voice, sounding steady enough, saying not to worry, Tilo could stay for as long as she needed.

Gutiérrez the healer, Eusebio's godfather, had been unconscious in the hospital for days. His wife had moved out a while back and he'd been living by himself. A customer found him lying on the porch of his shack, dehydrated and with a broken hip. He got taken to the hospital to die. Stick-thin, shrunken from the wine. They put him on an IV so he could drift out like he was dreaming.

That night, when Eusebio went missing on the river, the healer opened his eyes in the gloom of the ward. No one noticed because the other patients were asleep and so was the nurse on duty. Gutiérrez opened his eyes and saw his godson floundering in the treacly brown water. He didn't see him as he was now, a man, but as he'd been when he showed up that time with his pal who was dreaming about the Drowner. A kid in a growth spurt who already stank of cigarettes.

Well, I'll be damned!

Said Gutiérrez.

How'd I miss that?

Then he closed his eyes again and let himself be lulled by the splashing of his godson's arms as they gradually gave way to the river.

Tilo grabs his gear and sets off alone. Beyond the woods, a tongue of water winds through the grasslands, the flowering waxyleaf nightshade. It's ten in the morning and the sun is beating down on his bare back. He always misses his dad when he comes to the island. It must be that part of a person stays behind in the place where they die. There's a ton of photos of the two of them fishing together. He always brought him along. The last time, by total chance, he hadn't been able to come. One of his godmother's kids was having a birthday so he'd gone out to the country for the weekend. They'd spent the whole day swimming in the big metal stock tank. Marisa made them come out when the sun went down and their teeth started to chatter. Things got weird when they were out of the water. While everyone else, even the birthday boy, was getting dried and dressed by themselves, Marisa wrapped Tilo in a towel, gave him a rub, and kissed him on the head. It was kind of annoying and he squirmed free and ran off to join the others, who were playing at Indians around the fire. Marisa's husband had moved some embers to one side and grilled a few chorizos. That night no one said anything. They ate dinner and then turned in early. The next day, as soon as they were up, Marisa said they were heading back to town. Everyone protested, they were meant to have one more day of swimming and running around in the country. But Marisa cut them off, like she was angry.

Where the stream broadens out, he stops. Baits with a worm and casts. He likes that moment when hook and bait sink, the tiny hole they make in the water's surface, the gentle ripples that form.

First, that day, his godmother had left all her family at home. Marisa's children, who were like cousins to him, begged her to let him stay. And he wanted to, he said he could, he was allowed till the evening. But she said no, he had to go back to his mother. He joined in with his cousins' tantrums.

Pleeeease, just for a bit, don't be so mean.

They whined all together. Which normally worked, but not this time. Marisa snapped at her husband, just get the kids inside, ok? But at Tilo she smiled like she was someone else or rather the person she always was, sweet and kind as a teacher.

You can't stay today, little man, you have to go see your mum.

She stroked his hair and his cheek. Her eyes were damp and it scared him to see her that way.

He didn't know what was happening, couldn't even imagine, but he had a tummy ache. They made the journey in silence, him looking out the car window, his godmother's gaze fixed on the windshield. When they reached the hotel, he got out slowly, dragging his rucksack. His mother was standing in the doorway with folded arms. Marisa got out after him, though there was no need. His mum crouched down to give him a kiss. Her eyes were bloodshot.

Go on in, I won't be long.

She said.

Tilo went inside and turned back to look at them. His mother and Marisa were hugging, and although he couldn't hear a thing, he saw how his mother's back was shaking, and how the other woman didn't let go.

He doesn't remember the part where his mother tells him his father's dead. Did she use the word dead or did she say with the angels? Did she give any details or just say there'd been an accident?

Tilo was six. He was finishing first grade, he could read without stopping to spell out the words, his handwriting was big and kind of messy, and he was good at sums.

He doesn't remember that talk with his mother. Goes straight from the scene of Marisa and his mum hugging to the scene where he's crawling through pairs of legs that approach, pause, turn, retreat, and then slipping beneath the coffin. Unnoticed, he lies face-up on the floor and looks at the bottom of that wooden box. Apparently his dad is inside. Tilo shuffles along till his head's about level with where his father's must be. He'd asked why they couldn't look at him and his mum said his dad wasn't there any more. He didn't get it: was he there or not? And if not then what was everyone doing, hanging around a coffin with nothing inside it? If he wasn't in there, where was he? Had he been eaten by the fish?

They entered the cemetery behind the coffin, which was carried by El Negro, Enero and some relatives. Right away the cousins ran off to play among the gravestones. He wasn't allowed, he had to stay with the grown-ups. His mother held his hand so tight it hurt, and he had to ask her to let go a bit.

The hole was already dug. He saw, or thought he saw, some long pink worms poke out among the clods of fresh earth. Just right for bait.

The guys from the cemetery lowered the coffin with the help of some ropes. When it reached the bottom, they tugged the ropes free and pulled them back up. A couple of guys were waiting to one side, the ends of their shovels in the piles of earth. One of them looked at Tilo's mother.

Ma'am.

He said.

His mother stooped, picked up a handful of earth and gave it to Tilo, then pushed him gently to the edge of the pit.

Throw it in.

She whispered in his ear.

Tilo let the earth fall and then everyone else scooped up handfuls as well and threw them onto the coffin. His cousins ran over when they heard the thuds, and since by then everyone was leaving they started kicking the dirt into the hole, shoving each other and yelling. He wriggled free of his mother and joined in, laughing.

The line tightens in his fingers. A bite. That moment, the bite, the tug, the nervous excitement of a kid. He gets to work. Stands firm on the muddy shore. Raises his arm. Turns the reel. The fish fights. So hard it must be pretty big. He keeps reeling. It's hooked good and proper. He can tell by how it's thrashing on the end of the line. Finally he pulls it from the water. It glitters in the sun. Tilo smiles.

Might've known you were a wolf-fish, pulling like that.

He says.

The shop is a poky little room, just a few feet square. A chest freezer separates inside from out. Holed up behind it, the owner, an old man with grey hair and almost no teeth. Blue eyes, crisscrossed with red veins. The cigarette never dropping from his mouth.

The roof extends out, providing some shade between the shop and the street. Underneath it, a handful of tables. At the far side, a plank of wood held up by the same posts that hold up the roof. A bar to lean on.

Enero asks for some beers.

The coldest you've got.

He says.

The old man looks at him, scornful.

As if we'd sell warm beer here.

He says, raising his voice. Words jostling with the smoke from the cigarette that never leaves his mouth.

Enero shrugs slightly like a little kid who's screwed up. Asks for a couple of packs of cigarettes as well. And some ice.

When the old man's about to open the freezer for the beers and the ice, Enero stops him.

Hold up. First I'll have a quick beer here with the kid.

The old man opens the freezer all the same, grudgingly, for the beer.

The cold gets out if I keep opening it.

He says.

But this time he's just talking to himself.

He opens the bottle. Rude as hell. Doesn't even give them glasses.

Enero takes the cigarettes and the beer. Tilo waits, leaning on the wooden bar. The noonday sun sears the sandy street.

Under the roof, some islanders are playing cards and drinking wine.

Enero leans on the bar as well, looking at the tables and chairs. His enormous back, his calves and his ass are still in the sun. His head, bent forward, gets the shade. It's only hit by the glare when he tilts it back to take a long draught straight from the bottle.

That's more like it.

He says.

He squints. His throat, on the inside, cool as a fresh-cut aloe leaf.

That's more like it.

He repeats.

He passes the bottle. Tilo drinks.

Just drinks.

Not making a thing of it.

No one knows where the girls appear from, but suddenly there they are. First comes the smell of green grass given off by their long, newly-washed hair, still dripping at the tips, flowing and black as cowbird feathers, brushing the tops of their asses. The guys see them from behind, just like that, out of nowhere, buying something from the shop. The two girls stand in front of the old man, so they can't see him or hear what he's saying. One laughs and turns her head slightly. They catch a glimpse of her profile.

Enero nudges Tilo, who shrugs and brings the bottle back to his lips.

Eventually the girls turn around and they're even prettier in front than behind. Fresh-faced, no make-up. Not identical, aside from maybe their long, jet-black hair. One's taller and the other has bigger tits. Not identical, but very similar. Dressed like any other girls their age. Short shorts, jeans cut off with scissors, no hem. Their legs emerge, golden, the tiny hairs on their thighs shining like fish scales. And that smell of cut grass they both give off, from all over their bodies.

They look at the guys and smile. Enero smiles back.

Afternoon.

He says.

Can we have one?

Says one of the girls, nodding at the pack.

Nope.

Says Enero.

You can have two: one each.

They giggle, move closer. Taking the cigarettes, holding their faces to Enero's hand, to the blue flame of the lighter.

You're not from around here.

The other girl says.

Nah, we just came to fish.

Says Enero.

Oh, yeah? And what you looking to catch?

The same girl says and laughs.

Enero likes her. He likes cheeky girls. These ones are just kids, they must be what, fifteen, sixteen. But here on the island women grow up quicker than in town.

He snorts with laughter.

An old fella like me – what d'you think I'm here to catch? Except maybe a cold...

Our mami says you're as old as you feel.

Says one or the other or both. He doesn't know any more. His head's spinning from looking at them they're so pretty, like a trick of the summer light.

I'm Enero. And this here's my godson Tilo.

What kind of names are they.

Says one.

Enero? And where's Febrero and Marzo?

Says the other.

More giggling.

I'm Mariela and she's Luisina.

After my grandma. I know, I know, it's an old-lady name.

Says the one called Luisina.

But everyone calls me Lucy.

I'd offer you girls some beer, but that old tightwad didn't give us any glasses.

Says Enero.

That's okay, we don't drink.

Says Mariela.

Oh, really?

Says Enero.

Yeah, it goes straight to our heads.

Says Lucy.

I'm sure you still behave all right.

Says Enero.

I wouldn't be so sure.

Says Lucy and something flickers inside her.

C'mon, Mariela, Mami's waiting.

But Mariela can't stop looking at Tilo.

There's a dance tonight, just over there.

She says and points to an open space at the end of the sandy street.

That's the dancefloor.

Come on, Mariela, let's get going.

You guys should come, it'll be really fun.

C'mon, Mariela, Mami's waiting.

I'm coming!

Mariela pulls her arm free of Lucy's grip and winks at the guys.

Come. You won't regret it.

They turn and start walking. Again Lucy reaches for her sister's arm and the girl lets her. Away they go, intertwined, perfectly in step.

Enero watches them. After all, looking never hurt anyone.

One of the islanders playing cards brings him back down to earth.

Watch it with those two! There's poison in their pussies.

He says, twisting around without putting down his cards.

Enero looks at him, the smile still on his lips.

The islander winks.

Get a grip, pal, can't you see they're long gone? Long gone!

He roars with laughter and turns back to his game. His hunched shoulders soon merge with the other drinkers.

Tilo nudges Enero and makes a face, asking what the guy meant.

Enero doesn't answer and downs the last of the beer.

The air has suddenly thickened.

As soon as they're a little way away, Mariela presses close to her sister.

Oh man, I think I'm in love.

She says, nuzzling the other girl's shoulder.

Don't start.

Says Lucy.

But you saw how cute he is.

Mariela sighs.

They carry on down the sandy street. By then the ground is baking. They go barefoot all the same. Their hot pink painted toenails look like little macachín flowers.

Although they're a year apart and Mariela's the oldest, Lucy has always been more serious. Their mother says it's because hers was a bitter pregnancy. Things weren't going well with the two girls' father and he'd walked out before she gave birth.

You sucked up all the bitterness from inside me, she always says.

When they get home, their mother's outside, burning trash. So intent that she doesn't hear them open and close the gate. Lucy watches her a moment: she's wearing a saggy vest that used to be Mariela's and a faded skirt, her hair is tied back and she's stooping a little. Among the plumes of smoke she seems suddenly old. Lucy desperately wants to go up behind her and give her a hug. But her mami's not that kind of person and doesn't like affection. They'd had a big fight the day before and she'd said: Get out of my house, you little sluts!

The shutters in the room are lowered. Mariela flops onto the bed and fans herself with a magazine. Lucy lies on the bed next to hers, one leg stretched over the clean sheet and the other hanging down. A little smoke filters in through the gaps in the shutters but if they close them they'll die of heat.

Try the fan, see if it works.

Says Mariela.

Lucy gets up reluctantly and switches it on. The machine makes a rasping noise, but the blades don't move.

Here, have a go with this.

Says Mariela, tossing her a ruler.

Lucy pokes at the blades and it looks like maybe something but no. She keeps trying. In the end she gives up, turns it off and lies back down on the bed.

Mariela throws the magazine to the floor and shifts onto her side, one arm under her face, the other draped over the pillow. Lucy stares at the ceiling, notices a hole in the metal that's letting in a pinprick of daylight. When it rains it'll let in water.

Reckon they'll come to the dance?

Says Mariela, all hopeful.

Lucy doesn't respond.

Ever since they were little, they've had the habit of shutting themselves away in their room and lying on the beds to talk. It makes their mami angry. In the day,a because only slobs would lie around instead of helping in the house, getting a job or doing homework. At night, because the whispers and giggles keep her awake. She says staying up till the small hours is for whores.

I feel bad for Mami.

Says Lucy.

Mariela props herself up on one elbow, resting her cheek on her palm.

How come?

She says.

I dunno, just a feeling I had when we came home.

She's annoyed, that's all. She'll get over it.

Will we be like that when we have daughters?

Mariela laughs and rolls onto her back.

Listen to you. You'd better make sure you don't get knocked up or Mami really will lose her shit. As for me, I water my parsley plant every day, case I need it to get me out of trouble.

Lucy laughs as well.

You're so dumb.

She says.

Siomara stirs the fire with a long pole, nudging the trash to within reach of the flames. The pole catches alight as well and she bangs it on the ground to put it out. She rests her two hands on the end, and her chin on her pointy knuckles. She's thin, gaunt. When she gets undressed her tits hang down like two flaps of dry skin. She used to be curvy, full-bodied, attractive. Maybe not beautiful, but striking. Not so long ago, some men would still turn their heads when she went past. Now when they see her they lower their eyes, or look the other way.

She's always liked making fires. As a girl, if she fought with her mother or quarrelled with her brother, she'd go into the woods and make a fire. Or if she was really pissed off, she'd light one right there outside the family's shack. Lighting fires was her way of getting rid of the anger, pushing it out of her chest, as if she were telling them: look how big my rage can be, careful it doesn't catch you. And then one day it almost did.

She'd fought with her old man after somebody said they'd seen her screwing in the boat shed. Her dad, who was always liquored up, got back and just like that pulled off his belt and let her have it. She'd been taking a siesta and didn't understand. It was hot and she was in just a bra and panties, with no time even to pull up the sheet, the buckle coming down hard on her bare flesh. As he hit her he said again and again: I'll show you, you little hussy.

When his arm finally tired he dropped the belt and crashed out, to sleep off the drink, on the same bed where she was still curled up trying to shield herself from the blows. Trembling, she got to her feet. In the daylight outside, she saw the red welts on her legs and butt cheeks. She took a dressing gown of her mother's off the clothes line and covered herself. Then she gathered some dry branches and built a huge great fire, tall and bright. She built it near the shack and the tongues of flame soon reached the thatched roof. There was only her old man inside. Her brothers were at work and her mother was off visiting a relative. The neighbours showed up in no time and put out the blaze.

You stupid, stupid girl, you could've caused a disaster!

They said.

Then they comforted her.

She's been making fires a lot lately. Sometimes she can't find anything left to burn and goes looking for old junk that folks are throwing away and drags it home just to set it alight. Sometimes, if she doesn't feel like trawling through other people's trash, she burns a piece of furniture.

The neighbours complain.

Honestly, Siomara, I just hung that washing out and now it stinks of smoke.

They say, always respectful and a little frightened.

She doesn't even answer.

Before, she too used to give a crap. The clothes always immaculate. Doing the washing in the outdoor sink, scrubbing each thing a few times over with the bar of soap, rinsing and rinsing, drying it in the sun and during summer in the shade, so the fabric didn't crisp. When the girls were little she drove them crazy: don't get grubby, keep those socks white, those shoes spotless. As a single mother she didn't want to give people an inch, the girls always decked out in white, neat as a pin, with ribbons in their hair. Daring anyone to find anything wrong with her or her daughters. What an idiot! People can always find something. And if not, they make something up.

It wasn't her they saw screwing in the boat shed that time. Not that she didn't screw around. Of course she did! She was fifteen and the blood ran red-hot beneath her skin. But it was her friend Marita they saw.

Sometimes she thinks the fire talks to her. Not like a person does, not with words. But there's something in the crackle, the soft sound of the flames, as if she could almost hear the air burning away, yes, something, right there, that speaks to her alone. Even if it doesn't use human words, Siomara knows it's calling her. Saying: come on, you know you want to. Just like all the men she fell for, just like the father of her daughters, just like so many others. She answered those calls every time.

Why not? Who doesn't like a bit of attention? And every time, in the end, she'd climbed out of a window as if the building was going up in flames.

Come on, you know you want to.

It says.

She pretends not to hear. Still just about strong enough to resist. But for how much longer?

One day, she knows, she will answer the fire's call.

Aguirre lays a hand on her shoulder. Siomara looks around, leaving her flame-filled trance. She smiles at him, far away, gone.

Starting fires again.

Says Aguirre.

A fond rebuke, like you might make to a child or an old man.

He reaches for the pole and tosses it into the flames. Rolls a cigarette and hands it to her. Siomara takes a drag.

You eaten?

Says Aguirre.

Siomara searches for the answer with her gaze, somewhere in the distance. She laughs.

I can't actually remember.

She says.

Let's go to César's, they're having dorado.

Siomara shakes her head, resolute.

I can't! I have to wait for the girls.

Aguirre looks at her. Licks his finger and wipes a smudge of soot off her cheek.

C'mon, we'll go inside and boil some pasta.

He says.

The house is falling to bits. There seems to be less and less furniture. The walls need repairs, a lick of paint. The photo of the girls at their communion with two big bows in their hair, laughing, showing their crooked teeth, is the only thing adorning the dresser.

He, Siomara and their brothers finished growing up in that house. She and him were the youngest, and stayed on with their parents after the older ones built houses of their own or went off to the city to work. One day he built a little place for himself and moved out as well. Siomara went on living with their mother. She had the two girls by then and her husband had upped and left.

He has a mooch about while Siomara's cooking. The door to his nieces' bedroom is ajar. He stands for a moment looking at the crack, unsure whether to go in. In the end he doesn't, but he pushes gently and the door gives way, swinging fully open. The shutters are lowered against the heat, but the noon sun is still strong enough to light the room. His sister hasn't touched a thing. The two neatly-made beds, the floor fan, some posters of actors or singers on the wall. A pile of crumpled clothes on the chair, like someone had been trying things on in the mirror and then left them lying around.

Nearly ready.

Says Siomara from the kitchen. Aguirre closes the door and goes back to where his sister's straining the pasta.

The table is laid for four.

They eat in silence, staring at their plates. Aguirre finishes quickly. Siomara toys with her food, now and then bringing a forkful to her mouth, chewing, swallowing it down like a bitter pill. Aguirre rolls a cigarette and lights it.

Roll one for me.

Says Siomara.

Eat a bit more. You're skin and bone.

Siomara lets go of her fork and bangs on the table.

They're meant to be here for lunch! For fuck's sake!

She says.

She gets up, takes the pan into the yard and throws out the rest of the pasta. Then she begins clearing the table.

Aguirre gets up as well. He leans on the doorframe. Some dogs have found their way in to eat the scraps off the ground.

You know those guys who caught the ray. They fucking chucked it, can you believe!

He says.

But the only response is Siomara slamming her bedroom door shut behind her.

He stays where he is. Just over the road the woods begin. He knows them like the palm of his hand. Better than he's ever known another person. Better than he knows César, who's his friend. Better than he knows his sister, who's a mystery still. Better than he knew his nieces, poor things, they never had the time. He knows the woods better than he knows himself.

Some wind gets in between the trees and it's so quiet at this hour that the rustle of leaves could be the breath of a giant beast. He listens as it breathes. As it huffs and puffs. The branches move like ribs, inflating and deflating with the air that's sucked deep inside.

They're not just trees. Not just bushes.

They're not just birds. Not just bugs.

The quitilipi isn't a wildcat, though perched on a branch it might look like one.

They're not just any guinea pigs. It's this guinea pig.

This yarará.

This bromeliad, unique, its centre red like a woman's blood.

If he looks farther on, to where the road slopes down, he can just about see the river. A glint that makes his eyes water. And again: it's not a river, it's this river. He's spent more time with it than with anyone.

So.

What gave them the right!

It wasn't a ray. It was that ray. A beautiful creature stretched out in the mud at the bottom, she'd have shone white like a bride in the lightless depths. Flat on the riverbed or gliding in her tulle, magnolia from the water, searching for food, chasing transparent larvae, skeletal roots. The hooks buried in her sides, the tug-of-war all afternoon till she can't fight any more. The gunshots. Pulled from the river to be thrown back in later.

Dead.

Even though he's had lunch he still makes for César's. They'll have eaten as well but they'll be sitting around the table till it's time to go fishing.

He left Siomara asleep, fully clothed. Only her feet bare. He'd sat for a while on the edge of the bed, his back to his sister, till he heard her breathing slow. The same bed where their parents had slept and died. Their father first. He got sick: served him right. Then their mother, who went in her sleep like the blessed.

He didn't set off right away. He rolled a cigarette and smoked it slowly in the half-light, in the room's cool air. He remembered the siestas when he and Siomara were kids. The forays into the woods when their parents were asleep. Hunting small birds. Eating blackberries. Their brothers had moved away as soon as they grew up. Every now and then someone brings news of one of them. Interfering busybodies, because what's it to him? What does he have to do with those men he wouldn't even recognize in the street? What do they know about him, about Siomara? The same busybodies you get all over must pass on news of them as well. And those men who were once their brothers will listen like he does, more out of manners than interest. The two of them are all that's left of the family. When they die there won't be a single Aguirre left on the island. Which is the same thing as saying: in the world.

When he finally leaves the house, the sun hurts his eyes. The sandy streets are empty. Some kid running into the woods like him as a boy, escaping the siesta. The picui dove singing and that sharp kind of pain he gets in his belly every time he hears it.

As expected, everyone's under the awning at César's. Shirtless, shining with sweat and fish grease.

Playing cards. They've pushed the dorado scraps to one end of the plank they're using as a table. On some pieces of cardboard, the oily skins, the whole heads, the wide yellow eyes, shimmering in the siesta-hour sun. That same golden light envelops it all, as if radiating from the skins and charred scales. Two fish that had once been massive. Now: stripped bones and heads with open mouths, gasping for breath outside the water, inside a summer more massive than them. The same light envelops the men, who seem to tremble like a mirage, exchanging glances over their fanned-out cards, fingering the corners, their pupils glassy from the wine and heat. He approaches the light, approaches the awning. Silent and unseen.

But César, as if he smelt him, without looking up from his cards, says.

We thought you'd be here for lunch.

He says it like he's his wife.

I was at my sister's.

Says Aguirre.

How's she holding up?

Says César, one eye still on the game.

Oh, you know.

César isn't asking for the sake of it. Ever since he was a kid he's had a thing for Siomara. She went with everyone except him. Maybe because he was so close with her brother. Who knows how women think. Still, he doesn't hold it against her. When her husband left, he'd have taken care of her and the girls. Now, after the stuff with her daughters, and even batty as she is, he'd shack up with her if she wanted. He doesn't say that. Instead, he says to one of the guys.

Go in and get some bread.

There's none left.

The guy says.

How d'you know if you haven't looked!

Says César, banging the wooden board with his free hand, the one that isn't holding the cards.

It's fine, I already ate.

Says Aguirre.

But this punk's pissing me off.

Says César.

The guy laughs.

I don't know what you're laughing at! I was wiping your ass when you were a kid, so show a little respect.

Another guy puts down a card and wins the game.

César lays his cards down as well. Takes a swig of wine.

C'mon, pull up a chair.

He says with a wave of his arm.

Aguirre doesn't move.

I'm good.

He says.

You, get some more wine.

César says to the same guy he told to get bread.

The kid stands up, goes inside and comes back with the demijohn.

If you send him for wine he doesn't hang about.

Says César.

They all crack up.

Aguirre is handed a glass and he drinks, tilting his head slightly back. Then he wipes his mouth with his hand and rolls a cigarette.

César gets up and says he's done playing, but they can carry on if they want.

They all jeer because César's a sore loser.

But César ignores them. He hooks his thumbs in his shorts and pulls them up. The elastic snaps against his skin when he lets go.

Want to get in there? You'd beat those clowns with your eyes shut.

He says.

Aguirre shakes his head.

Instead, he says.

You know those guys who caught the ray.

Beautiful specimen.

Says César, though he never saw it, just heard.

They fucking chucked it away, can you believe?

Suddenly everything stops. The dealer pauses mid-shuffle. The drinkers put down their cups. Everyone looks at him.

They chucked it in the river!

Says Aguirre.

Motherfuckers!

Says César.

We need to teach them a lesson.

Says Aguirre.

What kind of a lesson?

Says César.

Lucy opens her eyes. She's covered in sweat. She was dreaming about the accident again. The bright sunlight is still coming in through the leak she saw earlier in the roof. She hears the hot metal creak. In the bed next to hers, Mariela is asleep. Her mouth partly open, the tips of her top teeth just visible; her arms by her sides, her head turned a little to the left.

The house is silent. A while ago she thought she heard voices and clattering pans in the kitchen. But maybe she dreamed that as well. Mami never has visitors.

She sits up in bed and looks at her fingernails. They've grown so fast! It seems like only yesterday she painted them and now there's a pale strip between the varnish and the rest of each finger. She'll have to touch them up before the dance. When was it? Tonight? Tomorrow? She doesn't even know what day it is. Her mouth feels dry, her breath sour. She gets up. It's so hard to get out of bed lately! She walks over the bare concrete to the kitchen and fills a big glass of water. She drinks till her belly feels tight. Then she runs the tap again and rinses her face.

Instead of going back to her room, she pokes her head around her mother's door.

Siomara, too, is asleep on her back, wearing Mariela's old vest and a faded skirt, her feet bare. Her bony chest rises and falls. Lucy lies down carefully beside her and watches her sleep. Her mami smells of smoke. Even when she's sleeping, her face doesn't relax. Her brow is furrowed, her jaw clenched. Her top and bottom teeth rub gently together. Wearing away like rocks. The white roots of her hair form a halo around her head. How can they need doing again? When it's just two, three days since she sat her down in the yard, a towel around her shoulders, and applied the dye, first the gross cream that smells of cat piss, then the comb to even it out, and then the shower cap. Maybe the only time her mother's features relax is when Lucy's colouring her hair. She remembers her face lifted to the late-afternoon light, her eyelids lowered, her forehead smooth. A slight pout of the lips, like she's smiling. And then, for a little bit longer, when she rinses her hair and dries it hard with the towel.

Lucy wants to be a hairdresser. She wants to give other women those moments of peace her mother seems to feel when she's doing her hair.

She lies on her back as well and folds her arms. When her grandma died they put her in this bed for the vigil, not quite where Lucy is but more in the centre, where there's now half of her body and half of her mother's. She and Mariela had climbed onto the bed and given their grandma a kiss. She was cold, like a doll's plastic face. Their mami had done her hair in a bun as usual. Come to think of it, their mami was also good with people's hair. She gave the girls trims and did their grandma's toner, not dye though, she didn't use that. The woman's white hair would be left bright lilac and then fade as the days went by. She used to cut their uncle's hair, too, and neaten up his beard. So hers is a gift passed down from her mother. And yet she always thinks she's too much like her father and that's why her mami loves her less than Mariela. When her mami stops being in a mood she'll ask: have you noticed I'm good with people's hair like you are?

Mariela opens her eyes. Lucy isn't in bed. She remembers they got back a while ago. She remembers the cute guy they met at the shop. She remembers there's a dance tonight and smiles because she'll see him. She gets up. It's scary in the silent, empty house, even though the sun's still shining. She goes into her mother's bedroom. Her sister and their mami are asleep. Or so it seems but when she gets closer Lucy half-opens her eyes and smiles, pats the bed and makes space for her. They're both still kind of sleepy and doze off together, curled up in each other's arms, by their mother's side.

Siomara opens her eyes. She doesn't know how long she's been asleep but she feels rested, lighter, her chest open. It's ages since she woke up feeling so good. Hardly moving, she reaches out and strokes the smooth patch of sheet beside her. Stares at the ceiling. There's no sound, aside from the little moans that houses make in summer. The zinc roof expanding in the heat. The comings and goings of the carpenter ants that drill into the wooden beams. The concrete floor creaking somewhere, a new crack beginning to form. The soft slow breath of her newly awakened body. She doesn't want to move and tip that delicate balance. She wants to stay there, on pause. Not thinking. Not remembering.

Enero, meanwhile, at the other end of the same island, of the same siesta, wakes up without further ado. He sees El Negro and Tilo set off in the boat, grow smaller against the silvery river, vanish around a bend. Him alone, under the aguaribay tree.

He planted one like this in his backyard once. Took it from here when it was still a sapling, just a couple of feet, and now it's a proper tree some heads taller than him. His mother would've liked sitting in the shade of its branches, sewing or reading magazines. He's always thinking of her: wouldn't Mamá have liked this or that, what would she have made of this or that, now if Mamá were alive today…

Does he think about his mother so much because he never had kids? Do folks with families of their own think less about what's gone before than about what lies ahead?

He almost had a kid once. A girl he'd been sleeping

with got knocked up and wanted to keep the baby.

Like I'd have a child with you.

Said Enero.

The girl had burst into tears.

Hey, hey.

Said Enero.

He gave her a hug to comfort her and they ended up fucking.

Afterwards, she fell asleep. Enero lit a cigarette and looked at her naked, splayed out on the bed. She wasn't ugly and you could see her tits had got bigger now she was expecting. He ran a hand over her thigh. Her skin was soft. Then he lay down on his back again and stared at his bedroom ceiling.

Delia was out with her friends at the bingo. It was a Saturday. His father, a travelling salesman, was away someplace in Corrientes. They never really knew where his old man had been till he got back. That night Enero was off to the dance with Eusebio and El Negro as usual. If the girl got her way and they had that kid, then his pals, his nights out, his fishing trips, everything would stop.

He got up, got dressed and shook her by the ankle. She woke with a smile and stretched her arms out wide like a child.

C'mon, up, my mum'll be back soon.

Enero said and went out to the yard.

In no time she was behind him, giving him a hug and resting her chin on his shoulder. He shrugged her off, annoyed.

Give me a few days and I'll sort it all out.

He said.

She went on smiling like a fool, not sure what he meant exactly, though deep down she knew there were just two options, or three.

Some days later Enero had found the money and stopped by her place to pick her up. As soon as she saw him, the girl's face fell. Enero gave her a quick peck on the cheek. His old man was home and had loaned him the car. They got in, one on each side, her with her head bowed.

Enero started the engine and patted her knee.

It's one thing having a bit of fun, and another to start a family.

He said.

The house of Gutiérrez the healer was pretty much as he remembered, though the part made of flimsy sheet metal had gone and now the whole thing was brick. There'd been a time when Gutiérrez had done well for himself. He'd had a local politician for a customer and the man had recommended him to his friends, all people with money to spend. Then the guy was in a car crash and ended up paralyzed. Gutiérrez had gone around boasting that with God's help he could make him walk. But God hadn't helped and nor had Gutiérrez, and nor had all the candles he lit or all the payé spells he cast. The man remained prostrate and the healer fell into disrepute. He had to go back to treating the poor, to curing indigestion, worming kids, and removing unwanted babies from their mothers' wombs.

The time they came about the Drowner, when they were kids, there'd been a whole crowd gathered outside. Now there was no one.

Gutiérrez's wife was waiting for them by one of the doors. Even though the whole house was brick now, it still had the porch running right the way along and a bunch of doors, all open except the one to the little treatment room.

The woman led them into the kitchen and asked Enero if he had the cash. He handed her the roll of bills and the woman counted it in front of them.

Right.

She said.

You wait here.

She said.

And you, come with me.

She said.

The girl followed her, miserable and ashamed.

Enero sat down and lit a cigarette. He wondered why there were so many doors and rooms if only Gutiérrez and his wife seemed to live there. A tabby cat sprang onto the table and let itself be stroked, arching its back under Enero's hand. Then it bit him hard and with another leap landed on the cupboard. From there it glanced back at him briefly and then, losing interest, began licking its paw.

After a while Gutiérrez's wife returned to the kitchen with the girl. Enero stood up, as a sign of respect for the woman of the house. The girl was staring at the floor. The healer's wife, however, looked him straight in the eye.

If you don't want kids then get the snip, okay?

She said.

They drove back in silence. The girl looking out of the window, dazed. Her hands clasped in her lap. When they reached her house, Enero tried to say something but no words came. And she didn't wait around, just opened the door and quickly climbed out. She went through the little wire gate that separated the house from the street without a backward glance.

Enero never saw her again. A while later he heard from a mutual friend that she'd gone to live in Buenos Aires.

Years later, when Eusebio said he was having a kid, Enero felt a twinge of jealousy and regret. There, for once, he could've beaten Eusebio. But the other guy always got in first. Even when it came to dying. That mystery was revealed to him before anyone else.

That night on the river has always been a blur. The argument over something that might've been true or might've just been a story someone spun Eusebio, he's never known which. Eusebio had been acting weird for a while. Slacking off and getting wasted more than usual.

The three of them argued and then Eusebio took off and they didn't see him for hours. He came back that night drunk out of his tree and wanted to go fishing.

But why did they let him get in the boat? Why didn't they stop him? Why did they let him go off like that?

He'll come back soon enough.

Said El Negro.

But he didn't.

How long was it before they started to look? To shout his name in the silent night? To realize he wasn't coming back, not then or ever again. Because they had to search the river and pull him out. All those hours later, all that way away. Potbellied, pregnant with the river, his open eyes seeking the light.

Mariela and Lucy lie on the dirty sand along the shore. A bunch of teenagers not much older than them are swigging beer in the water. They pass the bottle around, talking loudly and laughing. You can tell they're not from around here. They must be staying in one of the holiday homes on the island, a long way from the locals' shacks. The two girls know those houses because in winter, when they're empty, they sneak in with their friends to drink wine and smoke pot. They always steal some knickknack, an ornament, an ashtray already stolen from some hotel in a country they'll never go to.

As soon as the girls arrive and stretch out in the sun, the guys get rowdier to attract their attention. Dunking each other's heads underwater, jumping on each other's backs. Four gang up on one, drag him out of the river and roll him in the sand.

Mariela looks at the sky, more transparent than the water around them will ever be. Tonight, for the dance, she's going to wear her best dress. A dress she went to buy with her uncle in Santa Fe. First they crossed the river to reach the mainland. Then they took the micro. Leaving the island is always an event. They went through the underwater tunnel. All dark despite the daylight outside. The cars with their headlamps on. Her looking out the window though there's nothing to see, just concrete walls and marks where the water's soaked through. She didn't want to miss a thing. When they reached the terminal, her uncle said if she needed the bathroom that was her chance. He stood rolling a cigarette and browsing the covers of the magazines hanging in the kiosk. She headed for the bathroom. Walking slowly because she wasn't in a rush: she'd just pee, wash her hands, touch up her eyeliner. Some guys in the bar watched her go past and said something, quietly so she couldn't make it out. She likes feeling the men's eyes on her. A kind of heat that rises from her belly and makes her cheeks burn.

The bathroom smelled of piss and bleach. An old woman in a blue smock was tearing and folding strips of toilet paper. Mariela went to take one then remembered she didn't have any change. Just a big bill her mami had given her. So she thanked the woman, who glared back dull-eyed and went on tearing and folding the paper. She peed without sitting on the toilet. Half-squatting, she watched the amber stream flow from between her legs and hit the ceramic bowl. She found a scrap of paper in her jeans pocket and wiped herself before pulling up her panties. Once out of the stall, she washed her hands. The bathroom lady looked at her again, hoping she'd buy some paper to dry them. But she dried them on her trousers, then fixed her make-up and left.

Next up the shops on the pedestrian street, the choosing of the dress. Going in, trying things on, posing for her uncle and the sales assistants. He never offered a view.

Whichever you want, honey.

He said.

The sales assistants praised her figure, her waist. Asked if she'd thought about modelling. As they flattered her, they snuck glances at her uncle. Tall, upright, a fish out of water among the mannequins and hangers draped with fancy clothes, on a floor so clean and shiny it seemed more like the sky. Her uncle looked so funny, not knowing what to do with his hands, which were useless to him without a cigarette, rod, or fish knife. Wearing the clothes he only ever wore to leave the island: jeans, new espadrilles, his shirt tucked in. The women took in his brown neck, his leathery tanned arms, his black moustache, his narrow eyes. So different to the guys they must know.

They went in and out of various shops before she made up her mind. As they walked from place to place, she watched their reflection in the windows. Finally she found what she wanted. Her uncle took out the wad of bills and the sales assistant put the dress in a bag.

Before going back to the terminal they sat down in a bar. Her uncle had a beer and she had a Coke. There, too, people kept glancing their way. The men at the other tables and the ones at the counter. Looking at her with desire. At her uncle with envy.

The first night she wore the new dress she left the dance with a boy. She woke up in the woods when the dawn was a pink paper streamer among the trees. Her skirt all creased, covered in leaves and twigs. The boy was asleep beside her and she got up without making a sound.

When she arrived home, her mami and Lucy were sitting in the kitchen. Both looking like crap. Her mami stared at her for a long time without speaking. Then she stood up and said:

Go get some sleep.

In the bedroom, as she was undressing, Lucy grabbed her hair and gave it a yank. Then she hugged her tight.

You scared me, you idiot.

She said.

They got in the same bed.

Now tell me everything.

She said.

She half-opens one eye and sees Lucy chatting with the group of boys. Mariela laughs: her baby sister's coming out of her shell.

The night of the accident they'd snuck out behind their mother's back. Siomara was in one of those phases she sometimes went through, when she was grouchier than usual. Saying no to everything and dealing out punishments and bans for no reason. All because she could see how the two girls were growing, how little by little they were slipping away, how sooner or later they were going to leave her as well. She was afraid they might get pregnant or shack up with some bum. There was nothing she could do and it made her furious. That afternoon, the last afternoon she ever saw them, she'd flown off the handle over nothing at all. Unmade beds or clothes on the bedroom floor, answering back or something else that didn't matter.

Get out of my house, you little sluts!

She said.

And started collecting junk to set on fire.

She didn't see them leave. And she didn't look in their room till some hours later. The beds made, but the clothes dumped on a chair.

She stayed pissed off the whole rest of the day and got even madder when night fell and the girls still weren't back. She sat down at the kitchen table. Wanting to be awake when they came in the door so she could give them a piece of her mind. But eventually the tiredness got too much and she only woke up when it was getting light, her face resting on the table, her neck stiff, her nose inches from the overflowing ashtray. She checked the girls' bedroom again. They weren't there. She slumped down, fully dressed, on one of the beds.

After the bust-up with their mami, they swung by a friend's place for a drink of mate. They always did that when they'd had a big fight, made themselves scarce till she got over it. But there was no one at their friend's house, so they ended up at the shop. They asked the man for a couple of Coca-Colas on credit. He made them beg a bit. The old letch, always the same ever since they were little. Eventually he handed over the Cokes and a bag of crisps.

Who knows, maybe you'll bring in a few customers.

He said.

Mariela gave him the finger and the old man chuckled.

Cheeky little brats.

He said.

It was hot and the sun was still beating down on the zinc roof above the pavement. The metal tables and chairs were warm. The ground, studded with bottle caps from beers and fizzy drinks, glinted silver in the light.

They sat there doing nothing. Drank the Cokes. Finished the crisps and licked their fingers, which were covered in salt and grease.

They were about to leave when the group of boys showed up. Mariela knew the one they all called Panda, he was a friend of a friend of a friend. Panda recognized her and asked the girls to join them for a bit. The other two guys weren't from the island. They had some beers together. Every time the old man brought more bottles, he looked at the girls and said: careful now. The old fool.

It was getting dark when they suggested heading to a club on the mainland. They had the truck waiting, they could drive them to a dance in a town some five or ten miles away and give them a ride back later. Panda had a canoe, he'd paddle them across each way.

They weren't dressed up or anything, just in shorts, vests and sneakers. But the guys insisted they looked just fine, the dance wasn't fancy, they weren't planning on changing either.

Lucy liked one of the group and signalled to Mariela they should say yes. Mariela thought it would be no bad thing to be gone a few hours, make their mami worry a bit. Then next time maybe she'd think twice before throwing them out.

They had some more beers and set off when night fell.

The old man watched the group go as he cleared the table. Siomara's daughters had got prettier.

They crossed the river in two lots. When they were all on the mainland they piled into the truck. The girls up front with the guy who was driving. Panda and the other guy in the back.

The club was just a dancefloor in the middle of the countryside. A bar, a DJ, some feeble lights strung up under a metal roof. Kids from the nearby towns came in cars, in trucks, on mopeds, all the vehicles packed with way too many people.

Mariela and Lucy danced all night. Tipsy from the beers and a long way from home. Lucy made out a bit with one of Panda's friends, the one she liked. But she was more into the cumbia than the fooling around and the kid got tired of chasing her and went off with someone else.

At around five the slow numbers came on and the dancefloor began emptying out.

They went back to the truck. The driver, Mariela, Lucy and Panda up front, all squished together. And in the back, a few others who'd been stuck without a lift.

They chatted about the dance for a bit and then the girls nodded off. They opened their eyes when the truck was flipping all the way over in the air and plunging headfirst into the ditch. Deep mud and nothing else, just a few inches of water.

News of the accident reached the island at noon.

By then Siomara had gone out looking for her daughters, asking all the neighbours. The only one who could tell her anything was the old guy from the shop.

Yup, they'd been there, then they'd gone off with Panda and some of his friends. Panda, Canelo's kid.

Siomara went to Panda's house and he hadn't been home either. His mother didn't know anything. Not that she was worried. The mothers of boys don't worry about where they sleep or who with. Siomara made for her brother's place. Still angry, but as time went on and the girls still hadn't appeared, her anger was turning to concern.

Aguirre said they must've stayed over someplace, with a girlfriend most likely, and they'd be home soon enough. That she should come in for a drink of mate. Then they'd take another look around the island.

Siomara went in. She didn't want to be home alone and she wanted to believe her brother's words. While Aguirre was adding fresh leaves to the gourd, the news was announced on the radio.

A truck carrying people back from a dance had overturned in a ditch and they'd been so unlucky that the vehicle had buried them all in the mud. Nine of them. All dead.

There was no reason to think her daughters had been there. So she didn't understand when she was told, later on, that of the nine dead, two were her girls.

As well as Panda and her daughters, two other kids from the island were in the truck that overturned. They held a vigil for all five in a room at the Town Hall. The coffin lids spilling over with wild flowers. The irupé lilies had just come back out on the river. Two buds, one for each girl.

The three boys' mothers took over the room with their weeping. They hadn't been ready: women with sons are never ready for tragedy. Whereas Siomara didn't shed a single tear, not at the vigil which went on all night nor in the funeral procession along the river nor at the cemetery where the bodies were left forever.

The morning was crazily sunny. A gentle breeze rocked the raft that carried the five coffins, which was pulled along by two boats. Behind, in more boats and canoes, the families and neighbours. Some flowers came loose from the caskets and floated downriver, to be swallowed by swirls in the current.

Siomara was staring into the water. Every so often, Aguirre, who was with her, rolled her a cigarette, lit it, and put it in her mouth. She smoked till the embers burned her lips.

Although she'd seen her daughters' bodies, pale as the dawn, Siomara didn't believe that those badly nailed wooden boards could possibly contain her little girls.

She'd said as much to her brother. Her girls were somewhere around. They'd had an argument, stormed out and eventually they'd come back. She wanted to finish up here and get home as soon as possible to wait for them.

These poor people.

She said.

Aguirre looked at her blankly.

The poor things. How will they ever get over it?

She said.

Mariela gets up, brushes the sand off her back and goes to where her sister's flirting with the boys. Without saying hi or anything she grabs the bottle from one. Takes a swig. Spits it out.

It's warm.

She says.

The one who'd been holding the bottle grins.

Yeah, it's warm.

Mariela turns to her sister.

Let's go.

No, stay. We've got cold ones.

Says another.

We need to get ready for the dance.

Says Mariela.

You guys going?

Is that an invitation?

Says one.

Mariela laughs, shrugs. Takes Lucy by the hand.

See you around.

She says.

When Tilo and El Negro get back, they find Enero building a fire.

To scare off the mozzies.

He says.

And cook us some meat.

This one here wants to go to a dance.

Says El Negro.

To the dance?

Says Enero.

They invited us, remember.

Says Tilo.

Enero laughs and goes on snapping twigs with his hands and tossing them into the flames.

I dunno.

He says.

Now it's El Negro who laughs.

What's up with you? You never turn down a dance.

I dunno.

Enero says again.

Come on, let's do it, we'll be Tilo's wingmen. Seems he's got excited about the candidates.

Tilo laughs. Embarrassed.

I just meant, if we wanted to go out.

Enero says nothing, watching the fire.

Come on, just for a bit. See what's going on.

Says El Negro.

They walk through the woods in the darkness. Feeling their way. Everything so alive in there, and the three of them blind. Spiderwebs cling to their hair, to their faces.

El Negro says how one time in the woods in Corrientes, he saw spiders that live in nests in the trees. They spin these giant webs, with strong, stretchy thread. That day, he says, he saw them swinging from place to place in the woods, all riding on the web like it was a magic carpet.

Enero laughs.

Yeah right.

He says.

He stops to get out a cigarette. When he lights it, the flame looks like a giant blaze because the darkness is so thick. For some reason he remembers a painting in the house of some relatives that scared the crap out of him as a boy. Jesus with his chest opened up and his heart a ball of fire. Yowzer! Every time he went, it gave him nightmares.

The treetops grow vast with the night and you can only just see, every so often, a star or two, a patch of sky. Feet stumble over tree roots or ankles twist in loose sand. Now and then some gleaming eyes appear in the darkness then vanish: two tiny floating lights that flicker out. The sounds are sometimes sharper, sometimes softer, as they move through the woods. Creatures, birds maybe, all screeching together, frightened and threatening at once. A flutter of wings, tall grasses parting to let something through and then closing over behind. The silent watchfulness of spiders, insects and snakes. The ominous hint of yararás.

Enero can feel his heart racing, his friends' breath that's sometimes right up close, sometimes fading to nothing. All three have their arms stretched out in front, catching the branches, fending off scratches. They move like they're swimming, with short arm strokes, taking little gulps of air.

He's afraid. It's like something's following them and he keeps looking over his shoulder but all he ever sees is the woods. He wants to get out already, out of the sound of falling rain the leaves are making in the wind. Up ahead he thinks he can see moonlight.

Eusebio would've opened his eyes to a thick darkness like this when he was swallowed by the river. Would he have seen any light at the end? He remembers his bulging eyes when they recovered the body. As if just before dying he'd seen something so huge he couldn't take it in.

But what was it? Something too huge, that was for sure.

But also too terrible?

Or too beautiful.

When Enero finished at the police academy, he was posted to a little town right in the north of the province. In all his time there, half a year or so, he didn't see his family or friends, didn't go back home, and only called his mother a handful of times.

At the police station, if you could call it that − a room barely bigger than a security guard's hut, with an outdoor toilet − it was just him and the chief, a guy some years older called Arroyo. Amílcar Arroyo. He was seeing a girl who could've been his daughter and she was pregnant with his second kid. One day the girl came to bring them some food in a Tupperware box and when she left Enero's eyes followed her out. Arroyo noticed, smiled and said nothing could beat a tight little pussy, and that now the second kid was on the way, this one was losing its charm.

Still, only got myself to blame.

He said.

Shouldn't have trashed her so quick. But I like it bareback, what can you do.

He said and snorted with laughter.

Enero wondered what the girl ever saw in Arroyo. Without his uniform, Arroyo was just like any other loser in the town.

While they were eating the leftovers, his boss, as if he'd read his mind, said the town was full of girls in the market for real men like them. That he could help himself to any he pleased and no one would bat an eyelid.

That's how it goes here.

He said.

Enero replied that he wasn't planning on staying, so he'd better not get tied down.

Arroyo laughed again and started choking on a grain of rice he'd inhaled. Enero helped him, thumping his back and holding up his arms till he stopped. Once he'd recovered, Arroyo took a swig of wine, and red-faced, his voice still strangled, said.

Leave whenever you want. What are you worried about? Ties here are made of cobwebs... One little breeze and they break.

He didn't enjoy that time, though there was almost no work and they just sat on their asses all day. Arroyo was in everyone's pocket and they made good money turning a blind eye to cattle rustling and the roadside brothels that glittered, at night, like a string of fairy lights, along the length of Calle 14. There was no police car so they went around on horseback or on a moped seized in a minor raid that Arroyo forgot to record in his report.

He didn't enjoy it but at the same time he didn't

want to go back to his town, not even for a visit. Something bothered him about his new life in that backwater, and something about his old life, too, as if he were two different people with nothing in common but the feeling of not fitting in.

Arroyo soon took a shine to him, maybe because Enero did what he told him and never argued back. Not like the other little shits fresh from training they'd sent him in the past. Maybe that's why he even set him up with the kid sister of his missus, as he liked to call her, and put in a good word. Surely, he thought, with a tasty little morsel like his sister-in-law, Enero would stop wanting to leave. But a few months later, when he was offered a transfer to the police station back home (his father had pulled a few strings, but he'd never know that), Enero packed his bags. Arroyo was pissed off and told him to take the girl, that she'd got attached to him, that he'd better not leave her behind now he'd ruined her.

Enero held his arms in front of Arroyo's face, pressed his wrists together, and then pulled them apart.

Cobwebs, Arroyo.

At last they're out of the wood, sweaty and flustered.
They stop for a moment to take stock.
It's too dark to even see what you're saying in there.
Says El Negro.
Ha. Like you ever say much.
Says Enero.
Depends if there's much worth saying.
Says El Negro.
Let's stop and have a drink.

Says Enero.

He points to the white glow of the shop a few yards away.

They head over. The old man's sat alone at a table like a customer, with a pack of cigarettes, and his beer inside a foam sleeve. The fluorescent tube dangles from one of the beams that hold up the rickety porch. The electric hum and the insects hitting the light are the only sounds till they greet him.

Evening.

Says the old man, without getting up.

Can we get a beer?

Says El Negro.

The old man nods.

Don't see why not.

He says.

The three of them sit at the other table.

A litre bottle.

Says El Negro.

The old man turns his head and motions to Tilo.

Go on, kiddo, get one out the freezer. On the house.

He says.

Tilo glances at Enero and El Negro, who nod.

The boy goes into the dingy little room and comes back with the bottle and three glasses. When he puts them on the table, his fingers leave marks on the greasy glass.

What's this in aid of? You celebrating or something?

Says Enero.

The old man doesn't even look when he answers.

First one's free.

He says.

Much obliged.

Says El Negro.

The old man holds up his hand as if to say: Enough.

At first, when he was back in town, Enero didn't feel right. His mother and his friends were all as happy as if he'd come home safe and sound from a war. He wished he was as happy to see them. And he was, kind of, mostly. But at the same time he felt restless, like those flea-ridden dogs that don't know what side to lie on. He spent all day at the police station, and sometimes nights as well. There, with his new colleagues, inside his uniform, he felt less out of place than he did around the folks he'd known all his life.

In the months Enero was away, Eusebio and El Negro took to calling in on Delia for some mate. When Enero came back they carried on, though their friend was never there. One day Delia said.

My son's changed.

Eusebio and El Negro traded glances.

How d'you mean?

Said Eusebio.

I don't know. He's just different.

Said Delia with tears in her eyes.

El Negro patted her arm.

Nothing a bit of your cooking and some clean clothes won't fix.

He said.

Delia smiled.

I don't know.

She said.

He seemed strange to them too, but they didn't say anything, not wanting to worry her more. He was the same old Enero and he was someone else. They couldn't explain it. He was himself and he wasn't. He never talked about his time in that town whose name they didn't even know. At first they thought he was pining for some girlfriend he'd left behind. But when they asked him, Enero had creased up laughing.

A girlfriend!

He said.

What's up with you, dumbasses, you turn into fags while I was gone?

Then they began to get used to it. Or maybe they began to forget the old Enero, just like with time people forget the voices of the dead. If you asked El Negro now he'd tell you Enero has always been exactly the same.

Lucy is untangling Mariela's hair while her sister sits, wrapped in a towel, on the only chair they have in their bedroom. The radio's tuned to a music station and the windows are open because it's been dark a while now and there's a breeze. As her sister combs her hair, Mariela is painting her toenails. One foot resting on the edge of the chair, her chin on her knee, the tiny brush in one hand and the bottle in the other. Suddenly she stops and looks up, the brush suspended in mid-air.

Did I hurt you?

Says Lucy.

No. I just remembered I had a dream about Panda last night.

Who?

Panda, Rodolfo's friend. With the birthmark on his face.

Lucy doesn't know him. She carries on combing, thoughtful.

No, you do know him. If you saw him you'd recognize him right away.

Says Mariela.

And what happened in the dream?

I don't know, like I say I just had a kind of flashback. It was weird, there were lights and sirens.

But was he dead?

I don't know.

Because if he was dead and you remembered before breakfast it means he'll live longer.

Says Lucy.

Mariela puts the cap on the nail varnish and stands up

Wait, I'm not done!

Leave it, it's fine. I don't like people fiddling with my hair.

She takes off the towel and peers into the wardrobe, finds a thong and puts it on. Then she hunts for a bra to match. Lucy, meanwhile, untangles her own hair, looking out the window.

Did you make any plans with those guys?

Says Mariela, moisturizing her legs.

Which ones?

Says Lucy.

The ones from the beach, who else…?

Oh, no. I have no idea what we talked about.

Were you into any of them?

Lucy shrugs.

I'm never into anyone.

She says.

The night was getting started under César's awning. No one had got off their ass to go fishing. The afternoon was winding down amid rounds of wine, arguments over what lesson to teach the guys who caught the ray, with suggestions that grew more and more violent. From giving them a scare to beating them up to slitting their throats. As the wine flowed, the punishments hardened, and with them the avengers' tongues. As if they couldn't wait any longer, two of the youngest got into a fistfight. César went indoors and came back with a revolver. He fired twice into the air and the kids froze. With the gun still warm in his other hand, he gave each boy a slap.

What the hell are you playing at?

He said.

Then he sat down at the top of the table and placed the revolver in front of him.

We can't lose our heads!

He said.

He motioned for Aguirre to sit next to him. He rested a hand on his friend's arm and left it there and shut his eyes. In a calmer voice, he repeated.

We can't lose our heads.

They step into the woods, sure of themselves. The air damp from the night dew that rises off the river. Everything dark but they, like cats, move more easily in darkness. They know the name of each bird by its call, each tree by its bark, each plant by the size or texture of its leaves. Making their way through the woods as if through their own homes. They know where to tread so they don't disturb the snakes. So the scorpion doesn't sting. The woods have known them since they were yea-high. After all, more than one had been conceived and even born right here among the willows and alders, the espinillos and pink trumpet trees. With these same reeds and cattails for their cribs. Born and raised on the island. Baptized by the river.

César and Aguirre lead the way. No one says a word. All there was to say has been said already, under the awning. They each know what they have to do. Best not to speak so they don't get mixed up.

Aguirre is carrying the drum of kerosene. He wouldn't trust it to anyone else. These half-drunk oafs splashed it all over the container when they filled it, and as he moves his arm, the acrid smell pricks at his nostrils. Not far now. One last stretch of woodland and they'll be at the camp.

The dancefloor in question is a patch of land surrounded by polypropylene sacks, with a pole in the middle and strings of coloured lights extending out to form the shell of a roof. If it rains, it's all off. But tonight the stars shine in the clear sky and a crowd is gathering at the entrance. A woman at a little table takes the money and gives out numbers for the raffle. Someone asks what the prizes are and the woman grumpily responds: all sorts. Ladies get in free. There's a guy doing the music. On special nights they have a band. The regulars know the DJ's set off by heart. Always the same tracks, always in the same order. He only switches it up, on rare occasions, for a birthday, an anniversary, or if some girl he likes makes a request.

There's a bar selling fizzy drinks, wine, beer, and Fernet and Coke. And a grill doing chorizo rolls. On windy nights, the smoke blows onto the dancefloor and everyone curses at the chef.

Like you don't all live in houses full of smoke!

The guy yells back, offended.

Enero, El Negro and Tilo wait in line.

The beers they drank at the shop are taking effect. Enero, who at first hadn't wanted to come, is happy as a clam to see all the girls being let straight in, to see them strutting past the line of men, stumbling when their high heels catch in the sand. He nods in time to the beat pumping out of the speakers. El Negro and Tilo laugh.

This is the life.

Says Enero.

Siomara hovers on the fringes of the dance. Smoking and watching the girls who turn up. Thinking each one could be one of hers, but no. They never are. As soon as they get close enough they look nothing like her daughters. But from a distance they're all the same.

She makes for the bathrooms, which are outside. Two little huts, a bulb above each door, and a hand-painted sign that says: ladies gentlemen, with arrows showing which is which. The disinfectant smell mingles with the perfume and make-up. On tiptoe, she peers over the sea of shoulders waiting in line. In the crush around the mirror she thinks she sees Mariela's hair. She rushes forward and everyone complains.

Hey, lady, no cutting in!

She reaches out and her fingers are almost touching the long, loose black hair when the girl looks around. It's not Mariela. Siomara turns and retraces her steps.

She lights another cigarette. Walks among the cars parked in the empty lot next to the dance. There's movement inside some of them, music coming out of the open windows, giggles and moans. Siomara goes from car to car. Wanting to open all the doors and haul out girl after girl till she finds her daughters.

Where did she go wrong? She used to hate having to hide from her father to do what teenage girls do, so why do her daughters now have to hide from her? Why are all those girls hiding in the back seats of cars?

When they emerge from the woods, the camp is deserted. The embers are still warm on the ground where the fire used to be. The tents are up and they can see the boat beached on the shore. They rummage through everything. In a secret drawer on the boat, César finds Enero's revolver. He picks it up and gives it to Aguirre.

Look after this.

He says.

The youngest watch greedily as the gun changes hands, but they don't say a word.

At a signal from César, one unties the boat, pushes it clear of the shore, climbs in and begins rowing slowly. They watch him go. The moon lights the boat a silvery wake.

He should've set fire to it.

Says César.

Don't even joke, it's brand new!

Boats always come in handy.

Says Aguirre.

The two men turn back to the camp. César gives the order.

You.

He says to one.

Douse it all in kerosene.

The guy picks up the drum and starts sloshing it around.

The petrol smell soaks through the night.

When he's done, he throws the plastic drum aside.

César, sticking his chest out, goes to the porch of the tent and flicks his lighter. The flame quickly flares and begins to spread, following the trail of fuel.

The men take a few steps back and stand watching the little blaze.

For a while, just the fire. No one says a word.

Aguirre thinks of Siomara, of her goddamn obsession with setting things alight. He remembers the time she almost burnt down the family shack, and their father with it. The old man made it out that time because the neighbours got involved. But he knows it wasn't an accident. That the fire all came from inside his sister.

Every morning, since the girls died, he wakes up convinced he's going to hear that Siomara's set herself on fire. He's sure she'll do it. If she hasn't yet, it's only because she's lost her mind and thinks her daughters are still out there, that they'll come back one day when she least expects it. But he knows that deep down she knows. One day, the fire inside her will show her the truth. And then all that fire will come out.

César and the others look euphoric. Aguirre watches their shining eyes, their sweaty red skin. They look like woodland devils.

But no.

The devil doesn't live on the island. The devil, Aguirre knows full well, has to cross the river to get here.

The girls appear suddenly, out of nowhere, almost floating among the sweaty bodies shimmying on the dancefloor. The guys watch as they make their way over to where they are, near the people dancing but not near enough for them to be dancers as well.

Enero greets them with a toothy grin and elbows Tilo, who spills a bit of beer from his cup. Mariela and Lucy move closer to speak over the cumbia. The smell of fresh-cut grass envelops the group.

They introduce El Negro to the girls.

The girls to El Negro.

Enero dashes off to the bar and comes back with two bottles of Coke.

They toast to meeting again.

To the guys deciding to come.

To the girls not standing them up.

Let's dance.

Says Mariela and she grabs Tilo's hand.

Everyone!

Says Lucy, linking arms with El Negro and Enero.

All five step onto the dancefloor.

The catchy music sets them dancing in the current of moving bodies. They wave their arms in the air, clap their hands, the girls twirl from one embrace to another. All of them laughing. El Negro leaves the throng and comes back in a bit with some cider. The other four crowd around, the cork goes flying, they applaud and the foam gushes out. They drink it straight from the bottle.

Enero remembers another dance, the night they met Diana Maciel, Tilo's mother. Since he was the youngest, his colleagues always made him work the dances. Some because their partying days were over and they'd rather watch TV in bed with their wives. Others because their partying days had never stopped, and they told their wives they were on duty so they could spend the night with someone else.

For Enero, going to the dance wasn't work.

He liked acting the big shot in his uniform and on top of that he got free drinks. El Negro and Eusebio were there, as usual, just like before he was a cop.

They saw Diana when the dancefloor was emptying out. Later they learnt that she and her friends had come from a different party, and just swung by for a few more drinks before going home to bed. They weren't from the town. Or Diana was, but she'd gone off to study in Santa Fe and then been forced to come back because her father, who owned the hotel, had just died.

The three of them liked her right away.

Rosy cheeks, short hair, self-assured.

When the dance was over they asked the girls for a drink at a pool bar on the edge of town. There, Diana told them that she hadn't been back long, she was going to run the hotel, there was no money for her to keep studying. That she was bummed out. Her friends had come for a visit to try and cheer her up.

Within weeks, Eusebio was going out with her.

The one who was bummed out, when he heard, was Enero. He and Diana were friends by then and he'd thought he was in with a chance.

El Negro had laughed when Enero said Diana was just like other girls after all, nothing but a cocktease. El Negro had been quicker to adjust to always making do with Eusebio's leftovers. Then came the pregnancy, Tilo was born, and the pair split up. They were on-again, off-again for ages after that. Every time things were rocky, Diana confided in Enero. Eusebio knew, but he didn't mind. He'd rather she dish the dirt with his pal than with some randomer he didn't even know.

One of those times, and then more times after that, Enero and Diana wound up in bed.

They're sticky with cumbia and cider when someone grabs Tilo by the scruff of the neck and drags him away through the crowd of dancers, who glare but keep dancing like nothing's going on. Enero and El Negro are slow to react, and then comes the blow to the back of the neck, the pushes that send them slamming into those same dancers, who round on them too, their blood up.

What the fuck!

Coming in here, stirring shit up!

I'm gonna beat the crap out of you!

Lowlife scum, go back to where you came from!

Every time they try and turn around, the hands pushing them on push harder. The pair of them stumbling, flailing their arms this way and that so the people let them through.

Sonofabitch!

El Negro's eyes scanning for Tilo. He looks at Enero.

The kid!

He says.

I can't see him!

Says Enero.

Jesus Christ, what've they done with him?

Finally they reach the entrance. The people behind shove them so hard they fall flat on their faces in the road. When they manage to roll over, onto their backs, César jumps on El Negro and Aguirre on Enero. They straddle them and rain punches down on their heads. The men's ears are ringing and hot blood pours from their noses, filling their mouths like a sickly-sweet wine. They try to shield themselves with their arms, even throw the odd punch, which lands in empty space. When Aguirre and César's fists tire, when it's their own blood as well that's flowing from their knuckles, their pals help them up and give the men a few kicks in the ribs. Then one more each, for good measure, in the balls.

And don't let us see you round here again!

Says Aguirre.

He spits and wipes his face with his hand.

Some people have left the dance to enjoy the show. Gradually they go back in. On the dancefloor, the music's at fever pitch.

They stay on the ground a bit longer, the way foxes do, playing dead. When it all calms down, Enero squints out of his black eye. He reaches over and shakes El Negro, who moves slowly, moaning a little.

Where's Tilo?

They do their best to sit up. Although a few stragglers have hung around to watch, no one gives them a hand. A bit farther away, by the roadside, they see Tilo, sitting with his head between his legs, and the girls, who are taking care of him.

His nose is bleeding a lot.

Says Mariela.

He almost fainted.

They help him to his feet. El Negro pats him all over, checking for broken bones. Tilo says he's fine, just kind of dizzy.

You guys need to leave.

Says Lucy.

Maybe because the girls are leading the way or because they want to get the hell out of there, they make it through the woods much quicker than before. They don't mind the scratches from the branches, or the thorns that scrape their faces and arms. They don't even feel them. Their flesh all mashed up, numb from the blows.

On reaching the camp they find everything burnt to the ground.

Motherfuckers!

Says Enero.

The boat! Holy shit! The new boat...

Says El Negro.

Tilo looks around with tears in his eyes and doesn't say a word.

We'll find a boat to get you back across.

Says Lucy.

Come on.

She says.

They walk in a line along the shore. Lucy in front, then Mariela with her arm around Tilo, and behind them El Negro and Enero. Were it not for the fact that everything hurts, right down to the air coming in through their nostrils, they'd say it's a beautiful night. A slight breeze stirs the plants that float on the river and grow along its banks. The fish jump, looking for food on the surface.

A night like this, just like this, only darker. One of those times they'd come out here to drink with the excuse of going fishing. Eusebio was going crazy because Diana had sent a lawyer round to see him. It was months since he'd given her any money for Tilo.

What does she expect when there's fuck-all steady work right now?

He said.

And the bitch owns a hotel!

El Negro and Enero had offered to spot him some cash, enough to get him back on his feet. But Eusebio didn't want to know. The fishing trip was an idea they'd had to clear his head a bit. But when they arrived and it was getting dark and they started to drink, Eusebio got worked up again. It seemed he wasn't done talking about Diana Maciel.

What's more, the slut's fucking one of my friends.

He said.

Enero's blood froze. It was ages since there'd been anything between him and Diana, but even so. She could've told Eusebio just to hurt him.

Now hold up, Eusebio, listen…

He began. Eusebio cut him off and turned to El Negro.

And you, what do you say to that?

He said.

El Negro laughed and spread his arms wide.

Me?

He said.

What d'you want me to say. I've not heard anything.

You've not heard anything. But you know who's doing her. Say it. Say it to my face if you're such a man!

Said Eusebio.

Leave it out, Eusebio.

Said El Negro, draining his cup.

Stop being an idiot, we're here to have a good time. Not to gossip like women.

Enero had no idea what was going on, but just in case, in case Eusebio was talking about him, he said.

He's right. Let's have some more wine, Negrito!

El Negro went to the shore to get the demijohn and Eusebio stood up and yelled after him.

Go on, tell the poor bastard you're fucking her.

El Negro stopped in his tracks and slowly turned around.

Give it a rest, Eusebio, I've had it with your bullshit.

Before he'd finished speaking the other guy ran at him.

They both landed a few punches, but Enero soon got in between. Eusebio gave him a shove as well, while he was at it. Then he left.

It was getting dark. They collected some wood and lit a fire. They'd brought some fresh meat to throw on the embers. Enero wanted to know if El Negro really had been with Diana, but was scared he might end up confessing. He held out awhile then eventually asked.

Is it true?

He said.

El Negro looked at him.

You as well, dumbass.

He said.

It was pitch dark when Eusebio got back. He'd carried on drinking someplace else and was way drunker than when he left. He said he was going fishing, that this was a fishing trip so he was damn well going to fish.

Forget it, we'll go in the morning.

Said Enero.

The meat's almost done. Have something to eat and get some rest. Tomorrow we'll set out early.

He said.

Eusebio looked at him, then grabbed his stuff and got in the boat all the same.

Leave him.

Said El Negro.

He'll come back soon enough.

Lucy and Mariela help them into the boat. Tilo looks like a sick puppy. Enero's a wreck. El Negro, more or less in one piece, pushes the boat with the help of the girls then clambers in and takes the oars.

Now get out of here!

Says Mariela.

Get out of here, since you can.

She says.

They stand on the shore, waving them off, till they merge with the night and disappear. From the boat the whole island is a single black shape, ruffled by the treetops.

Enero puts his arm around Tilo and pulls him close to his aching body.

It's okay, son. It's okay.

He says.

When Lucy and Mariela get home, they find their mami waiting up for them in the kitchen. She's smoking. The ashtray is full. They kiss her and she smiles.

Sweet dreams, darlings.

She says.

They get into bed. They're so tired. Like the princesses in the story their mami used to read them when they were little: they danced all night till their shoes were worn through and in the morning they fell sound asleep. They don't even talk like they usually do.

Mariela is out in no time. Lucy is slower to drift off. The last thing she sees before her eyes fully close is the fire blazing in the backyard.

TRANSLATOR'S NOTE

When Selva Almada is interviewed in the Spanish-language press, one question she's often asked is how on earth her translators manage. The language of her books is so steeped in her small-town upbringing in the Argentinian province of Entre Ríos that even people from Buenos Aires joke about needing to read her with a dictionary in the other hand – not that the words she uses can be relied on to appear in dictionaries, or indeed in online searches. 'I always tell my students that to be a writer you need to have a good eye,' she has said. 'But as for me, I think I have a good ear.' She's right: her work is defined by her ability to capture the patterns and rhythms of everyday speech and turn them into spare, perfectly-weighted poetry.

I first encountered Selva's work through her previous novel, *Brickmakers*, the second in a loose trilogy of books linked by their exploration of masculinity, beginning with *The Wind that Lays Waste* and ending with *Not a River*. *Brickmakers* tells the violent and ultimately tragic tale of two rival brickmaking families – a tale that we hear backwards from the novel's opening scene, in which the two eldest sons of these families lie sprawled in the grass of a deserted fairground, bleeding to death after a knife fight. The book is set in the dry, dusty north-eastern province of Chaco, and the characters – and narrator – speak in a combination of '80s and '90s slang from Chaco, Entre Ríos and the working-class suburbs of Buenos Aires, along with a smattering of more literary language. The resulting prose has a visceral, lyrical intensity that matches the harshness of the sun-baked landscapes where the characters live their lives.

In *Not a River*, Selva takes this literary project further, removing everything extraneous – speech tags, chapter divisions, even most of the words – to bring her prose to the very brink of poetry. The novel takes place in another masculine world, this time telling the story of three men on a weekend fishing trip to an island in the Paraná Delta. However, the lush, green landscape couldn't be further from the parched earth of Chaco. The line breaks and lack of chapter divisions make the text itself river-shaped, its short sentences lapping at the silence like waves on the shore. And the Entre Ríos slang, here, is woven into a kind of soundscape filled with echoes and sighs, as befits this dreamlike narrative in which the boundaries between past and present, and living and dead, become increasingly blurred. 'The very universe of the novel ended up telling me how it should be written,' Selva has said. 'In a murmur, almost like the sound of the water.'

★

So, how on earth *do* her translators manage?

When I was originally sent the Spanish manuscript of *Brickmakers*, I wondered if this world of illegal greyhound races, bar-room brawls and swaggering male bravado, populated by characters who spoke in such unfamiliar ways, was simply too far from my own – should I, I wondered, step aside and make way for another translator, someone who was more at home in Selva's world? But the problem – aside from the fact I didn't know any greyhound-racing translators – was that I was already hooked. The rugged beauty of the prose had got under my skin, and I knew I wanted to take up the challenge. Perhaps I didn't have these voices at my fingertips yet, but that didn't mean I couldn't go looking for them. I resolved to teach myself to speak as these characters would, gradually piecing together the ways that English would behave in their mouths.

This was the first time I'd gone looking for voices in this way. I read the English-language writers who influenced Selva – such as William Faulkner, Carson McCullers and John McGahern – and anyone else I could think of who used oral language in interesting ways, from Irvine Welsh to Flannery O'Connor. I learned some handy tricks from translations of other slang-heavy texts, for example those by Frank Wynne, Julia Sanches, Sophie Hughes, Ellen Jones and of course Chris Andrews, whose excellent translation of Selva's first novel, *The Wind That Lays Waste*, showed me what was possible. I also watched WWE wrestling videos on YouTube (thank you, The Rock) and sought suggestions from the users of online motorbike forums (thank you, Eagle Six, oldenslow, hogcowboy, Porky and Motogrady).

When I began work on *Not a River*, I realised I'd have to go looking once more. I worked my way through a stack of fishing memoirs and novels, from Hemingway's *The Old Man and the Sea* to David James Duncan's *The River Why*, a wonderful account of a life spent fishing the trout-streams of Oregon, which taught me not only a good deal of technical jargon, but also about the silence and slow, meditative coexistence with the river without which fishing would be impossible. I spent whole afternoons on fishing forums, reading blow-by-blow accounts of users' struggles to land particularly troublesome catches. With both *Brickmakers* and *Not a River*, however, my greatest debt was to Cormac McCarthy, whose books showed me again and again how to strip a sentence back to the bone.

My aim, as I collected these words and phrases for *Not a River*, was not to construct voices that sounded as if they were from any particular place – I didn't want to turn Enero and El Negro into Oregon trout-fishermen, for example. Instead, I was seeking to piece together a language that was earthy and colloquial, as natural as breathing, and could plausibly feel like the way people might speak on this island in the Paraná Delta. For that reason, I also chose to leave some words in the original Spanish, as well as to follow Selva in including words like 'camoatí' and 'curupí' from Guaraní, an indigenous language with considerable influence on the Spanish spoken in this part of Argentina. As these terms mingle with the English, the translation becomes a soundscape of its own. How pleasing, for example, to place a sturdy Germanic monosyllable alongside some assonant Spanish, and describe a character's bare feet as 'plump as empanadas'. And what a thrill to hear the half-rhyming Argentinian names echo in their new surroundings, when Eusebio goes missing on the river and people back home wonder: 'What if the rumours are wrong, if they've got the wrong guy? / If it's Enero. / If it's El Negro.'

★

When Selva is asked how her translators manage — and by now her work has been translated into a dozen languages, among them Norwegian, Japanese, Turkish and Greek — she generally replies that she has no idea, but that she finds it reassuring how many questions they ask her. I find it reassuring that she finds it reassuring, because during my work on *Not a River* I asked plenty. What kind of animal, for instance, was a quitilipi, since there wasn't a single Google result for it? (Answer: an owl that often gets mistaken for a wildcat.) I'm very grateful to Selva for all the patient explanations, sometimes accompanied by photos of disconcertingly feline owls — and grateful, too, to have been trusted with these extraordinary books.

Annie McDermott
August 2023

CHARCO PRESS

Director & Editor: Carolina Orloff
Director: Samuel McDowell

www.charcopress.com

Not a River was published on
90gsm Munken Premium Cream paper.

The text was designed using Bembo 12 and ITC Galliard.

Printed in November 2023 by TJ Books
Padstow, Cornwall, PL28 8RW using responsibly
sourced paper and environmentally-friendly adhesive.